Claus and Effect

PIPER RAYNE

Cover Design: By Hang Le

1st Line Editor: Joy Editing

2nd Line Editor: My Brother's Editor

Proofreader: My Brother's Editor

About Claus and Effect

Two strangers who couldn't be more opposite find themselves on an unexpected cross-country road trip days before Christmas where whatever can go wrong, does.

He's an Army Ranger.
She's a baker.

He's organized and rigid.
She's messy and carefree.

He doesn't do relationships.
She's following her heart.

His family chat blows up his phone.
She just buried her last living relative.

The holiday season doesn't seem so jolly as they venture from one mode of transportation to the next. But, they have to become friends and rely on each other if they're going to survive all the obstacles thrown their way.

As the miles grow shorter, vulnerabilities are shared, and by the time they reach their destination, neither one of them is sure what they really want for Christmas anymore.

Claus

AND

Effect

Prologue

Her energy emanates through before she fully steps into the room.

She's the reason I'm here tonight. I don't do a lot of parties anymore now that I have a regular clientele, but something whispered to me that I needed to be here tonight. So when I received the invitation to do readings at this swanky Christmas party on the Upper East Side, I agreed. One never goes against one's spirit guides.

My gold bracelets clink together when I extend my arms for her to sit in the chair across the table from me.

I slide the tarot cards over as she takes her seat. "Shuffle these and separate them into three piles."

Her hands shake, her fingers struggling to keep a grasp on the edges of the cards.

"Relax, darling."

She shoots me a small smile.

"What's your name?" I ask.

"Tessa." She divides the deck into three, and I stack them together to begin the reading.

I dish out the cards in pyramid formation, each one telling me something. It's clear why the universe put her in my path.

She's lost.

"You've had a hard road. There's been a lot of loss in your life."

"Yes," she says, not elaborating, as if she's afraid she'll give me information to use.

"There's a recent loss that has caused your physical energy to weaken, your aura to dim."

She nods. "My great-uncle passed away, and there was a guy I was dating, but—"

I raise a hand, shaking my head. "Not a person. Something else. Career?"

She blinks rapidly, finally, she's starting to believe me. "Um, yeah... I just closed my bakery. Never got it off the ground."

I bite down my smile, not because I'm happy she's been dealing with so much, but because I think she'll believe what I have to say now. Act on it.

"I see the cloud above you that's been weighing you down, lifting. But you must be open to it and allow your heart to override your mind when warranted. You have trust issues."

"Doesn't everyone have them? This is New York City." She gives me an empathetic smile.

I nod. "A lot, but if you want to find fulfillment and happiness in life, you will have to open yourself."

I read her cards further. "This man you said you were dating—"

"We weren't serious."

"You give up on men easily."

I close my eyes, trying to picture him. I look to my right, pushing through the fog. An image emerges. He's just as lost as she is. "I see him now."

"Who?"

"Your soulmate. Dark hair, his family welcoming you into their home."

"Um..."

"He helps people." I squint, his entire being becoming clear. "West coast. He's headed west. You need to head west, too."

"But... we were only casual."

I put up my hand to stop her, the feelings too strong to be interrupted. She's definitely the reason I'm here tonight, to guide her to listen to her own intuition.

"When you show him how much you care, he'll admit his own feelings. You both might have some faults, but if you work through them together, you will have everything you've dreamed of."

"Carter?" she says in disbelief.

"I can't see a name. But this man is your one." I open my eyes and stare into hers. "Listen to the universe, Tessa. It's never quiet. Be receptive to what it's telling you and you'll find where you belong."

"Okay, thanks." She digs out a twenty and pushes it across the red crushed velvet tablecloth. "That was fun," she says as if we played a carnival game.

I stand from the chair, my last attempt to get her to listen to me. "Tessa," I call out to her. She turns back. "Don't ignore the signs. I see you with his family on Christmas. This is your chance. Your happily ever after is waiting, you just have to take the first step. Have faith."

She gives me a little wave before pushing her way back through the hanging curtain in the doorway. I'm no Santa Claus, but if she listens to me, she'll receive the best gift one could wish for—true love.

Today is the first day of what will change the trajectory of my life. At least, that's what the psychic told me. And I'm choosing to believe her because what else do I have to lose?

Andrew pulls the car up to the curb of JFK Airport, him and my best friend Kenzie's hands entwined over the center console. The happily married couple.

"Sorry for breaking up our throuple this Christmas," I joke, but since they are basically my family *and* my social life, I'm deflecting with humor.

Kenzie glances back from the front seat. "Are you sure you want to go? We don't know how legit the psychic was. I mean, she was at a Christmas party."

"I don't want to take the chance."

Had I planned to chase Carter to his parents' house, even though his invite was a pity one? No. Mostly because I have no money to my name. Then Andrew left a first-class ticket to Portland in their guest room this morning, along with a note that read:

I never thought I believed in this love stuff. Two years ago, I fell in love with an elf. Go explore what could be, and if it doesn't pan out, at least you tried.

Merry Christmas,
Andrew

And he's right. What do I honestly have to lose? I had to close my bakery and I just buried my great-uncle, the last living family member I had. What's wrong with hoping for a little magic during the holiday season? Some might call me crazy, but I'm going to follow my gut and hopefully at the end of this journey, I really will get my happily ever after. Besides, the psychic told me to watch for the signs and Andrew gifting me with a plane ticket seems like a big one.

"Andrew, you have to be aggressive." Kenzie reaches over and lays her hand on the horn to signal to the person in front of us who's taking forever to pull back into traffic to get a move on.

"It's the holidays," Andrew says in his posh British accent. "You're supposed to be cheery."

But looking out the window at the crowded sidewalk packed with luggage and people, anxiety stacks inside of me.

This is it. Now or never.

Andrew and Kenzie continue to bicker as we file out of his car and they go to the back to retrieve my bag. I step on the sidewalk and stare at the airline sign.

You're nuts, I tell myself. But then I glance back to Kenzie and Andrew, finding his arms around her and his lips on hers. Who would have ever thought they were right for each other? No one, that's who. But they fit perfectly, and Carter *was* a nice guy. I just never gave us a chance to get there, but now that all changes.

I take my bag from Andrew.

"Be careful and call us if you need us." Kenzie throws herself at me, wrapping her arms around me so tightly I look at Andrew to unglue her from me.

He laughs. "She's not your baby going off to college, Kenz." He guides her back by her shoulders to stand next to him.

"I'm really doing this." I nod.

"You really are," Kenzie says, biting her lip.

"I'm proud of you," Andrew says, smiling over at me.

I nod over and over again. Andrew smiles. Kenzie's eyes are lined with fear.

"Okay, I'm going now." But I don't turn around.

Come on, Tessa, turn around. You can do this.

Forcing any more debate from my thoughts, I turn and step forward, only to trip over a bag. I step to my side to try and right myself but hit a man's shoulder, which catapults me forward, my foot catching on the sidewalk seam and I fall flat on my face.

This is not a good sign, universe.

I lift my head and look up to see the military duffel I initially tripped over swung over a guy's back as he saunters into the concourse.

"Oh, Tess." Kenzie rushes to my side like I'm her new kindergartener on the first day. "I can't believe he didn't apologize." She narrows her eyes in his direction.

"I'm not sure he saw me," I grumble, dusting salt and snow off my jacket. "I felt like a pinball."

No one around me is paying any attention. Of course, because we're at a New York City airport one week before Christmas.

"Still." Kenzie continues to glare like a mother might. I wouldn't know since mine died when I was young.

"All right, if I don't go now, I'm never going to go." I hug her once more. Quick and tight otherwise I might never gain the courage to do this.

Andrew lifts his hand in a wave that turns into a thumbs-up with a big cheesy smile.

I'm sure he's anxious to be free of me. I would be if I were him.

"Go to your husband. I'll call you."

I release her, grab the handle of my suitcase, and walk steadily into the concourse without looking back. But I feel her watching me as if she's just waiting for me to run back to her.

I walk to the self-serve kiosk, check in, get my boarding pass, drop my luggage off, and walk toward security. As we all stand in line, moving inch by painful inch, I continue to glimpse at my watch.

I don't fly a lot but airports always suck. I take a deep breath, the anxiety gaining the longer I stand in line. I close my eyes and envision where I'll be soon—in a plush first-class seat where they probably give you champagne before takeoff.

Since it's a later flight, I hope to curl up with a blanket and watch a movie I've had no time to watch recently. Oh... or binge-watch television. The anxiety dissipates from every tense muscle just dreaming of it. I open my eyes and my gaze floats up and attaches to someone else's. A man's blue eyes meet mine. His are like the surface of the ocean in the Caribbean. Strong shoulders... then my brain stops processing as I realize he's wearing military fatigues. I have no idea if he's the soldier whose bag I tripped over. I'd expect many military personnel to be heading home for the holidays. Those on leave at least.

He doesn't react to my attention but continues to step forward. When he reaches the front of the line, I'm only two people behind him. A security person takes him to a new line. Thank God they're opening a new line. No more waiting.

I step forward, only to run into the back of the woman in front of me. She scowls and throws a warning look over her shoulder.

Okay then.

The woman proceeds to one line and I go to the other, everyone scrambling to take their electronics out of their bags, empty their pockets, remove their jackets, and take off their shoes. For a moment, I succumb to weakness and look in the direction of the soldier. He's being searched with his shoes on and his duffel on the ground. Guess he's getting special treatment.

He shoots me a cocky grin and winks. I draw back. Does he think I like him? Well, I mean really, what's not to like? Carter's face comes to mind quickly, reminding me what I'm doing here—I'm traveling across the world for a man and that's not him.

After a horrible experience at security where I make an utter fool of myself by forgetting to take off my cardigan and my watch, all I want to do is eat and then get to my gate.

My phone rings and I put it to my ear, grabbing all my stuff and finding a bench.

Another bill collector. Great.

I put my shoes and cardigan back on, my watch, and then grab my purse and bag, desperate to eat so my stomach stops growling.

I spot a pretzel place. Perfect. It will tide me over, but I'll still have room to eat all the yummy food they serve in first class.

I've never flown first class before, and I can't wait to see what all the fuss is about.

I'm busy on my phone, scrolling through Instagram, seeing my friend's decorated trees while "Last Christmas" plays over the speakers of the airport. A few parents passing by are exasperated by their kids. And then there's the odd person who just looks happy. Like they're living in the moment, but most are practically jogging and weaving between people.

"Next," the woman behind the counter says.

I pocket my phone. "A pretzel with salt and a lemonade, please." I smile at the woman, already able to taste the pretzel on my tongue.

"Oh, I'm sorry, we just sold the last one." I turn to my left and my jaw hangs open. Damn, GI Joe strikes again.

"Okay." I look at the case to see what's left, but I really don't want a pretzel wrapped over hot dogs.

I point to the case and before I can even get my question out to ask if that's all they have left, the woman says, "Uh-huh."

My stomach growls, but I don't want to be sick on the plane and the last time I had a hot dog, I ended up with food poisoning. "No thanks, I'm going to pass." I walk away from the counter.

I check the time. I have no idea why we have to be here so early.

Trying to keep my mind off my trip, I go to grab some sweets for the plane and a bottle of water. Of course, GI Joe is in there, perusing magazines. He takes one and a pack of gum, going to the checkout girl who's been staring at him the entire time. I get it. I would too if I weren't already on a mission.

Finally, what feels like a lifetime later, he leaves with what I think is her phone number on the back of the receipt. I don't know why that irks me. Because he's got that hot macho military thing going on? What do I care, I don't even know the guy.

Maybe I'm just wound up tight and more anxious than I think. I just need to get on that flight, get my butt in that first-class seat, and relax.

I checkout and the girl working appears to be on cloud nine, practically giddy, texting her friends while we wait for my card to go through. My dead great-uncle's wallet weighs heavily in my purse. The only inheritance I have left between him and my parents is what's in there. Which I promised I wouldn't touch unless I had to.

Once I'm in the hallway, I find my gate and sit by the window, staring out at what I'm assuming is my plane. I people watch and finally my anxiety and questions as to whether I'm doing the right thing start to diminish. The psychic was so adamant this is where I need to be to find where I belong.

"Tessa Atwater, please report to gate B27 immediately. Your flight is boarding," rings out over the airport speakers.

I bolt up in my seat and look at the gate sign where I'm sitting. B20.

Oh shit. They must have changed the gate on me.

I grab my stuff and run down the terminal, hoping like hell my happily ever after doesn't fly away without me.

Chapter Two

I arrive at gate B27, and the long line that's normally formed when people are waiting to board a plane isn't there, and the entire seating area is cleared out. The ticket agent is looking around with an annoyed expression.

I rush over to where the woman is getting ready to shut the door.

"Wait!" I shout. "I'm Tessa Atwater."

She stops and gives me an expression as if to ask where the hell I've been.

"I'm so sorry. I was at the wrong gate." I scan my ticket and the machine beeps.

She gives me a wan smile. "You need to board the plane now, ma'am. Everyone is waiting."

I cringe and walk down the corridor, where there's no line of people waiting to get on the plane. *Shit*.

The first flight attendant I meet glares and asks me to quickly take my seat.

"I'll be quick," I whisper, hoping to get on her good side, but she just makes a noise and goes back to whatever she was doing.

I read my seat number off my ticket once more. "4B," I mumble.

I kind of wish I could have a window, but I'm not going to complain. It's first class. I didn't even pay for the ticket.

As I walk down the aisle, I stare at the seat numbers above the seats. I get to row four, ready to crawl into my seat, but someone is there.

"Oh," I say, staring down at GI Joe in his fatigues.

The same GI Joe who received special treatment in security, took the last pretzel and probably the one who tripped me with his bag.

Irritation flares inside but I give him a sweet smile and say, "I think you're in my seat."

He raises both eyebrows at me and shifts his weight to the side, digging into his pocket to retrieve a printed-off boarding pass. While he's busy, the lady next to him looks me up and down in judgment.

"4B is me." He holds his boarding pass out toward me.

I hold mine up. "Me too."

"Well, if you weren't late and holding up the whole plane, princess, maybe you'd have gotten here first," he whispers, clearly not about to get up.

My head rears back. Did he seriously just say that? "Sorry, we don't all run on military time."

"Is there a problem?" A flight attendant comes up behind me.

"GI Joe and I both have the same seat number on our boarding pass," I say, lifting mine.

She smiles at him and purses her lips at me, yanking the boarding pass from my hand, then delicately takes his. She huffs while looking over them both. "I've never seen this before. Hold on." She walks up the aisle and the entire first-class section groans.

Some of them already have blankets over them, drinks in

their hands. I should've been first, GI Joe is right. The flight attendant gets on the phone at the front of the plane while I stand there feeling like everyone looking at me thinks I'm trying to scam my way onto the plane or something.

I'm so irritated now that my dream of traveling in first class might be ripped away from me. And by the same man who has already caused me so much irritation all day.

He's probably one of those people who everything magically falls into place for. God, what must it be like to have that be your life? I'll never know, mine is the exact opposite.

"Don't get up or anything," I snip.

"Oh, I should get up because that's the chivalrous thing to do?" He raises his eyebrows.

"It's the polite thing to do."

He unbuckles his seat belt and stands in the aisle, crossing his arms.

I can't deny, his arms are impressive even covered with his jacket. "By all means, sit. You're the woman, so you should have the seat, right?"

My cheeks heat. "Meaning?"

"Now you're distressed *and* naïve, princess?" He raises both eyebrows.

Do his soldier buddies pluck them? How can they be so perfect?

"Tessa Atwater, correct?" A different flight attendant comes up to me, the flight attendant who took my boarding pass behind her.

"Yes, that's me." I manage to slap a smile on my face.

"We'd been trying to get a hold of you prior to boarding but you didn't come up to the desk when paged. I do apologize, but first class was overbooked and since yours was the last ticket sold, we had to move you to coach."

"Coach?" I screech like an entitled bitch when in reality, it's where I always sit.

"Yes." She smiles sweetly.

"But...my boarding pass?" I eye the woman who took it.

The attendant hands me another piece of paper. "This is the right one. I do apologize and you'll of course be refunded the difference between the two."

My shoulders slump and I stare at GI Joe, who's snickering and sliding back down onto the seat with the assumption that this is just it.

Why can't I ever get a break? The more I look around at everyone in first class eyeballing me, the more my self-pity morphs into anger and my temper rises to the surface. The lion inside me purrs, sharpening her claws.

"So, I'm the one who gets screwed?"

"If there was anything we could do, we would. On behalf of the airline, we do apologize," the attendant says. "And now if you could take your seat in the back. I'll store your bag up here as a courtesy because there are no overheads open back there." She reaches for my bag, but I don't give it to her.

"Right, I get shoved back there even though I had a perfectly good ticket. And of course, if I say something, I'm the asshole, because he's in the military and fights for our freedom."

I ignore the few gasps around me because the lion inside me is roaring now.

The soldier straightens his back and grants me his full attention with a smirk so big I'd like to slap it off. But getting arrested will only make this worse.

"Ma'am, it's been a long day and I know the holidays can bring a lot of emotions to the surface, so why don't you take your seat so the plane can take off?"

"Sure, I'll go stuff myself in the small coach seat because, let me guess, the middle seat was the only one left?"

"Ma'am." She's trained well. Her voice hasn't risen one octave so far.

16

I bring my hand to the bridge of my nose. "Why would I expect any different considering how shitty life has been lately?"

"I'll have to escort you off if you don't take your seat," she says, voice sterner now.

I drop my hand and narrow my eyes at her. "Really? You're going to escort me off when it's your airline that double-booked a first-class seat?" My hands are moving in all directions.

"This is your last warning," she says.

I close my eyes for a beat, then turn my head sharply toward the soldier. "Enjoy first class."

"I most definitely will." The edges of his lips tip up and I glare at him.

I'm not sure if it's in my head or not, but I swear I growl and stomp through the curtain from the serene section of first class to what looks like a kindergarten room in coach.

Fuck my life.

The flight attendant follows me, and sure enough, I'm in the second row from the back. At least I'm on the aisle.

"Thank you for understanding," the flight attendant says, taking my carry-on.

I slide into my seat and stare at the round, pregnant belly of the woman beside me. Beyond her in the window seat is a grandma with an open tin of cookies on her lap. I buckle in and fight back the tears that are desperate to fall.

The more I sit, the angrier I become. Not just at the first-class situation, but at everything that's been weighing heavily on me lately. Then I think of about a million things I should've said to that jerk who was in my seat. I hate it when that happens.

"**M**an, she's a bitch," the woman next to me says once the whole scene is over.

I don't enjoy being a part of a spectacle, especially when I'm in uniform. People won't hesitate to pull out their phones and videotape or snap a damn picture these days. "Traveling is stressful. Holidays are stressful."

My phone dings in my hand and I click on the family group message, happy to have an excuse to stop talking to this woman, though not so happy about the messages. My family is treating my coming home as if I was injured or a POW.

Mom: Can't wait to have you home. We'll be at baggage claim.

Lil'Bro: If anyone questioned whether you're Mom's favorite, it's been confirmed. Wait until you see the spread.

Lil'Sis: There's a reason he's her favorite. He's not a douchebag who can't put the toilet seat down.

Me: Shit, did you fall in?

Dad: The scream in the middle of the night confirms it.

Lil'Sis: So great sharing a bathroom with him.

Mom: Tre doesn't need to hear us gripe. He's been through enough.

I shake my head because she has no idea how much I miss the banter of my family. I'm thankful to get to experience it.

Lil'Bro: Get home so I can school you in rummy. I'm the leader right now.

Lil'Sis: Because you cheat.

Lil'Bro: I do not cheat.

Lil'Sis: Really? Say it with a straight face.

Dad: We miss you, Tre, tell the pilot to fly faster.

Me: They're not really big on cockpit visits these days. We're pulling back from the gate. See you in five hours.

Mom: ☺

Lil'Bro: Prepare yourself. There will be tears.

Me: I'll text you when I land.

I really hope there aren't poster boards in my family members' hands when I meet them in arrivals. I'm not sure why my anxiety is at an all-time high with the thought of seeing them. They're my family. The ones who have missed me most. Maybe it's returning home, to my friends and the memories of before I left.

"I just don't get people like her. I mean, as if she should get the seat over you?" The woman next to me starts up again now that I've put my phone on Airplane Mode and pocketed it.

"She's probably having a bad day."

I feel like a total ass for treating her as if she was out of line. The seat was hers. She paid the money. When the attendant at check-in offered me a first-class seat as a thank you for my service, I assumed they had an open seat, not that I was taking someone else's. But her writing her phone number on the back of my boarding pass should've been my sign.

The more attitude the brunette gave me, the more I gave it right back because that's what I'm used to. I've spent years with soldiers who razz each other endlessly. If you don't hand it right back, you're considered weak. Things just escalated from there. I shouldn't have fed into it.

I lean my head back and close my eyes as the flight attendant goes over the safety procedures in the middle of the aisle. Rather than drifting off to sleep, all I can picture is that woman's dark hair thrown in that messy ponytail, her bright blue eyes showing how she was moments from tears. I know the flight attendant said her name, but I didn't catch it, and I wish I did, though I don't know why.

I'd tracked her back at security. As I was pushed to the side and checked with someone looking through my things and patting me down, she was the entertainment for the area. At first she forgot to take her sweater off, so she rushed back, apologizing to everyone she was inconveniencing. Then her Apple Watch was still on her wrist. The security guy had to tell her to take it off and put it in the tray.

Exasperated as she was, she did that move women sometimes do when they blow the hair that's hanging in their eye away to see better. I'm not sure what it is with that move, but it always turns me on. Once she was through security, her arms were full of all her things and she went to a bench and tossed it all in her bag, then slipped her feet back into her shoes. At least she didn't put her shoes at the end of the line, holding everyone up like some people do.

Her phone rang a minute later, and she disappeared from sight. A woman like her, it was probably her boyfriend. Likely whoever will be meeting her in Portland. No chance a woman like her isn't single.

Eventually I drift off. I'm not sure how long I'm out for, but when I wake, we've taken off and it's still dark within the cabin. A few people have their lights on above their seats and are reading or working on their laptops. I stretch, pulling back my shoulders and glancing at the woman next to me. She gives me a welcoming smile as if she's been either watching me sleep or waiting for me to wake up.

"Good morning," she says, wiping some pretend drool from my face with her thumb.

What the fuck?

I must give her a confused look because she laughs, apparently getting the whole wrong impression. "Just kidding, it's still nighttime."

I rub my eyes, still getting used to having a good sleep.

"So, tell me about yourself," she says. "Do you just not wear a ring or are you not married?"

The woman is attractive, a few years older than me from what I can judge. She's nice enough I suppose, but I don't want to discuss my personal life with some stranger.

"Not married," I say in a gruff voice.

"Oh, Carly owes me a drink." She wiggles in her seat in celebration.

My forehead creases. "Carly?"

"The flight attendant." She points at the short-haired brunette who was rude to the woman who was supposed to be in my seat. "You were sleeping, and we got to chatting."

"Oh." I think I'd rather be back in coach right now. "I have to use the bathroom." I unbuckle myself and slide out of my seat.

"You'll have to go in the back. The bald guy from the first row has been in there for twenty minutes already."

"Great," I say and sneak past the curtain that separates the first class from economy. I take a moment for a deep breath, gaining the distance I need from my seatmate.

I can kind of see why the woman was so upset to be moved back here. There are kids whining, people talking. Overall, it's much more social back here.

My eyes scan over the seats as I make my way to the back, but I can't find the brunette from earlier. She's probably sleeping, and she hates me anyway. I'm halfway down the aisle when the brunette from earlier gets up from her seat near the back. I bite my lip so I don't smile when our eyes meet.

Maybe she's going to apologize. *I* should definitely apologize. My mouth opens as she slides out of her row and steps in front of me. She quickly turns her back to stand in line for the bathroom in front of me.

"Excuse me," I say.

She glances over her shoulder then turns around. "Oh, did you want to use *our* bathroom?"

I look up to see both of the bathrooms are occupied right now. "First class is taken so..."

"So, you're okay using the bathroom but not sitting with us common folk?"

So much for apologizing. This woman is infuriating. "It wasn't my fault the tickets got messed up. I'm not sure why I'm getting your wrath?"

"He's a hottie," a senior woman says from the row the brunette came from. "Want a cookie?"

A tin hits my stomach, and I look down at a pregnant woman in the aisle seat who's holding the tin containing a crap-ton of decorated cookies. "They're so good. I've had five already," the pregnant woman mumbles, and I watch crumbs fall to her chest.

I hold up my hand. "I'm good, thanks."

"Suit yourself." She shrugs and gives the tin back to the grandma who has her silver hair pulled back in a clip.

"They're for my grandkids. My son moved them across the country from me and this was the first Christmas I had to make and decorate them all by myself."

"I'm really sorry. It's hard being away from your family during the holidays," I say. I know how much it sucks not to be with your loved ones this time of year.

The brunette in front of me huffs, drawing my attention back to her.

"What?" I arch an eyebrow.

She shakes her head. "Nothing. It's just that you'd think if you were really military, you'd miss a home-baked sugar cookie."

"You think I'm not a real soldier?" I chuckle.

"I'm just saying it's weird."

"Maybe I'm diabetic." I raise my eyebrows.

"Are you?"

"No."

"Well then." She eyes the tin then me again. She's hot, but I'm starting to think she might also be a tad unhinged.

"So what? Because I don't want a cookie, I'm not a soldier returning home for Christmas?"

"It's like a movie. You return home and, on the flight, run into a snarky brunette you secretly want."

I look down at the voice and the pregnant woman smiles brightly as if she thinks the brunette and I are going to walk out of the Portland Airport hand in hand singing Christmas carols. Not a fucking chance.

"Polly, I already told you, there's nothing remotely romantic between us," the brunette says.

"Because she's going to Portland for the other guy," the grandma adds.

My muscles tense. Other guy? Jealousy should be the last emotion overtaking me, but... what's with this other guy?

She looks at me, and for a moment, the chip on her shoulder is gone. There's a vulnerability shining inside her. She did not want me to know about this. "It's just... I mean..."

I raise my hand. "It's none of my business."

"A psychic told her she was going to die alone if she didn't," the grandma continues, and the brunette sighs.

"Psychic, huh?" I have no idea what to think of that.

She knocks on both bathroom doors. "Can you please hurry?" She turns back to me and crosses her arms.

My eyes dip to her breasts for a second but meet her eyes again before she gives me a black eye. Rightly so.

"You don't seem the type," I say.

Her fiery eyes land back on me. "Pathetic, you mean?"

"I just meant the type to follow a guy."

"So then really pathetic?"

"Jesus, I can't say anything right according to you." I shove my hands in my pockets. When will these people get out of the bathroom? I just need to go to the bathroom and sit down in my seat for the remainder of my flight and nod off. Once I land, I'll never see this woman again.

"Well, that's probably because your mouth is moving and you're speaking." She gives me a saccharine smile, then turns her back to me and shifts her weight from one foot to the other.

"So, where are you back from?" the pregnant lady asks.

"Sorry, it's classified."

"Of course it is," the brunette says. I can practically feel her rolling her eyes in front of me.

I lean forward and lower my voice. "I'm an Army Ranger, so most of my missions are classified," I whisper in her ear, and I swear goose bumps trail down her neck.

She guffaws. "Might as well have said you were a Navy SEAL."

"Since I'm wearing my 'fake' army fatigues, I felt as if Ranger was the better option. This trip at least."

She turns to look at me over her shoulder, and I wink at her. Her nostrils flare and she gives me a look as though she wishes she could kick my ass, but we both know she'd lose.

"Hard work." The pregnant woman reaches for my arm. "Thank you for your service." Then her hands rub her belly. "We both thank you."

I nod and mouth, *thank you*. I hate scenes like this, while this woman obviously loves them.

Finally, the bathroom door opens, and the man who comes out is pasty with a tinge of green to his skin. A rancid smell follows him out, and everyone around us chokes.

"Oh my god, I can't." Polly, the pregnant woman, stands

and squeezes past us, rushing into the bathroom. A second later, we hear her puking.

The other bathroom door opens up, and again, the woman coming out is pasty white and sweating.

"Honey, I think the fish was bad," the man says.

She holds her stomach. "I agree."

The flight attendant escorts them over to the staff area, offering tea and throw up bags.

"By all means, ladies first?" I say to the brunette.

"Oh, now it's ladies first." Her hands land on her hips. "Please, I insist. After all, your service keeps me safe. Think of it as me repaying you."

"So generous. I didn't get your name."

"No need to exchange names. This should be the last time I'll have to interact with you."

She slides by me, and I purposely make it difficult for her, causing her tits to press against my chest. I tell my dick to simmer down, that he's only reacting because it's been too fucking long. She sits down in the middle seat, and I wait a moment before holding my breath and walking into the bathroom.

After I've gone and washed my hands and am walking back to my seat, I stop at the end of her row, leaning in to avoid waking anyone. "It's all yours, princess. Sorry about the pee on the seat. Turbulence." I straighten and head back to my seat.

"Now calm down, Tessa, you're going to give yourself a heart attack," the grandma says as I walk away.

Tessa.

I smile to myself.

Chapter Four

TESSA

"I think you're missing your opportunity with that one," Polly says, leaning over into the aisle to watch him leave.

I grab a snowman cookie from the tin and bite off the head, crumbs flying everywhere. "He is so not my type."

"Honey, he's everyone's type," Gladys says.

"The ass on him," Polly says, using her hand to fan herself.

"That's how you got that in your belly." I point at her swollen stomach playfully. After I was sent back to coach, I offered to switch seats with Polly because she looked so miserable in the middle seat. The middle seat sucks, but I can't imagine flying in her state.

"Who knows what my parents are going to say." She stares at her belly as if it's a crystal ball.

"They're going to love the baby." I smile at her, and she returns my smile, though it's a little sad.

According to Polly, the father of the baby didn't want anything to do with her after she got pregnant, so she's going home with the hopes that her family will help her. I hope they realize how lucky they are to have her and a new baby. So many people take their families for granted.

Out of nowhere, she grips my hand.

"Polly! That hurts." I look from our hands up toward her face.

Her eyes are scrunched closed, and her other hand cradles her stomach.

"Are you okay, sweetie?" Gladys asks, leaning over me to get a view.

"I don't think so. I think it was a contraction." She cringes and fear shines in her eyes.

"Oh, sweetie, it's Braxton Hicks. You're too early for that." Gladys waves her off and picks up her book again, adjusting the light above.

"Eight and a half months is too early?" Polly asks.

"What? I thought you were six months pregnant?" I whisper as if it matters at this point.

"Well my belly isn't that big, so I just said that in order to get on the plane. I couldn't drive, and the thought of a bus or a train, being that uncomfortable for that long... I couldn't do it. I need to get to Portland as soon as I can."

She's so young, probably twenty, so I don't want to offend her, but I want to cry out, "Are you insane?"

"Okay. It's understandable." Naive, but understandable. "Labor can take a while."

"I was in labor with my no-good son for eighteen hours." Gladys turns the page in her book that I'm thinking she's not really reading.

"Then maybe this is—" Polly grips my hand again, crushing my fingers together.

"Another one?"

She nods, her face turning beet red.

"Breathe, Polly."

She releases her breath right in my face.

"Oh, they're close together." Gladys shuts her book and shoves it in the seat pocket in front of her, then unbuckles her seatbelt and leans toward us. "We need to see if she's dilated."

"What?" My eyes widen and I look back at Gladys. "Want to switch spots?"

"I wish I could, but why do you think I don't crochet anymore? Arthritis." She holds up her hands.

"So, me?" My stomach turns over on itself.

"Unless there's a doctor here." Gladys says it loudly enough that a boy hits his dad in the shoulder two rows up.

Relief unwinds all the tension in my body. Thank God. No checking out someone's vagina for me today. Things are looking up.

"I'm a dentist," the man says. He looks at his son. "I take out teeth, not babies, bud." His hand lands on his kid's hair and he ruffles it.

The little guy, who's now standing on his seat, eyes us as if we're his best entertainment. "Sorry. Do you need a tooth taken out?"

I smile because this kid is the only reason I'm keeping it together right now. "No, but who knows by the end of this."

"Is there a problem here?" The flight attendant glares at me, then looks at my hands on Polly's stomach and her face slackens. "Please tell me you're not in labor."

"You could be nicer about it." I give her my best evil eye.

She continues to stare at Polly, who answers with a whimper, tucking her chin into her chest and squeezing her eyes tight.

"Keep squeezing my hand," I whisper. "As hard as you need to."

She does exactly that and I pretend not to be in pain, pressing my lips together to keep from grimacing.

"How far along are you?" The flight attendant's tone is concerned, bordering on panicked.

31

"What's done is done," I say. "Her contractions are close together—she's having this baby."

She stares at us for a beat.

We haven't been in the air that long. There's no way we're making it to Portland with this baby in Polly's stomach.

"Let me talk to the pilot and see if there's a doctor on board." She spins on her heel and hurries toward first class. "I swear, it's always crazy with the holidays but now this woman gets on a plane about to deliver," she mumbles loudly enough that Polly hears her.

Tears swell in Polly's eyes, and I rub her shoulder.

"Don't listen to her. Just... let's unbuckle you." It's then I notice she's not really buckled in. She pretended to be.

"I couldn't get it around me, and I didn't want to draw any attention." She looks so young and innocent. I can't imagine having a baby back when I was her age.

I nod. "It's okay, don't worry about any of that."

Static comes over the speaker, then one of the flight attendants gets on and asks if there's a doctor on board. Wherever she is, someone must say something because she says thank goodness and hangs up the phone.

"I think there's a doctor. Great news." I give Polly my most reassuring smile.

"Yes, great news. This way you have a professional looking at you down there." Gladys chimes in with her thoughts. "You wouldn't want just any man doing it. There are perverts out there, you know?"

I glance over my shoulder at Gladys. "Maybe it's a female doctor." Then I turn back to Polly. "Just hold on, they should be here any moment."

She nods, but she's not saying much, just breathing. Then she signals for me to get closer.

"You okay?" I ask in a quiet voice.

"What if I go to the bathroom?"

"Do you have to?"

She shakes her head, looking exasperated at me. "When I push, what if... in my Lamaze class, they said it's more common than uncommon for..."

"What?" I'm trying to think back to my health class, but there's too much going on around me to remember anything from Mr. Carmichael's class except the vision of him rolling a condom onto a banana. I swear to God, the first time I saw a guy roll a condom on, that's all I could think of. It's a real mood-killer, let me tell you.

"What if I shit myself?" Polly says a little too loudly, and Gladys laughs behind me.

"Oh, honey, doctors are used to it." Gladys waves off Polly's concern.

"I'm on a plane," Polly whines and looks at me, as if I can do anything to help. I have no control over any of this.

"The pilot would like updates as you have them." The flight attendant approaches, and I blow out a breath of relief.

"Oh, thank goodness," I say, but as she walks past, GI Joe appears from behind her. "You're not a doctor."

"I was a medic." He bends down next to Polly, completely ignoring me. "How far apart are your contractions?"

"I don't know. They're close."

He stares at her for a beat, clearly thinking.

"Shouldn't you be checking her blood pressure or something? Checking her out down there? Something? Anything?" I say.

I eye between her legs and Polly squeezes them shut.

"Sweetie, he's definitely been between a lot of women's legs, don't be shy." Jesus, Gladys just can't help herself.

"I'm waiting for Angie to get me the medical kit," he says, meeting my gaze.

Of course he knows the flight attendant's name. He probably has her number too. I don't know why the idea bothers me.

"How nice of her."

"Can you two please just get along?" Gladys asks. "The girl is scared, and she's having a baby. She doesn't need two people bickering around her as she brings her child into this world."

I stare at GI Joe, who's now only in a gray T-shirt that says ARMY in big black bold letters, and I try to ignore the way the fabric stretches along his shoulders and biceps. The man can fill out a cotton tee to perfection.

"Fine," I say.

He nods. "Agreed. Okay, Polly, I'm going to take your pulse." He lifts his arm, which holds a watch with so many gadgets on it that it looks as if it could fly this plane. He places two fingers on her wrist, and he studies the watch while counting to himself. It's kind of cute the way his lips move but he doesn't speak. "Okay, good."

Angie rushes the medical bag over, and he takes out the blood pressure machine, holding it up for me to see. Everyone surrounding us watches him work from his knees to the side of Polly. He straps the cuff around her arm and takes her blood pressure.

As he removes the cuff, he says, "Blood pressure is great, just keep those breaths even and steady. Now, I have to see if you're dilated. I know this is uncomfortable, especially on the plane." He looks around, assessing the area.

I can reluctantly admit to myself that he's probably a great soldier, able to think fast on his feet.

"How about you two come out, lift the armrests, and Polly can lie across all three seats?" He looks at Angie. "Grab me a couple blankets."

"Sure." She rushes to the back, and he turns to me.

"I'm thinking we'll make a tent over the seats. Maybe

you crouch down by her head to lend her support. And your other friend can make sure no one sees her from behind me."

"Gladys," she says, introducing herself to him.

He nods and spares her a smile. "Nice to meet you."

"Bet you wish you would've taken a cookie now. Sugar rush." She slaps him on the shoulder.

"Adrenaline will have to get me by." He looks up and our eyes meet, his lips tip, and for a moment, I forget what a jerk I think he is.

"Here you go, Sergeant." Angie comes by, and I'm immediately reminded that we're actually at odds.

We get to work draping the blankets over the seats, a makeshift fort like we're kids, while Gladys holds a blanket up behind him so none of our nosy neighbors get a good view of what's going on.

"I can't believe I did this. I'm so stupid," Polly says, tears streaming down her face. "I can't even keep her safe. I should be in New York."

I run my hand along her forehead. "Stop it, you're going to be a great mother. You were trying to get home to your family and there's no harm in that."

She continues to cry as I attempt to reassure her.

"Polly, I'm going to lift your dress now," he says, telling her every step until he stills and looks up at me. Since Polly is only propped up with a small pillow, she can't see his look of panic. "Okay, um. Give me one second."

He stands and I peek out of the ceiling of blankets to see him walk to the back where the flight attendants are standing around. One is on the phone with who I assume is the pilot. I don't know what he's saying, but they have a look of fear after he's finished.

He returns to us and puts on another set of gloves from the medical kit. "Polly, you're fully dilated and the baby's head is crowning, so we're going to push, okay?" His voice is gentle and calm.

I would be a complete mess right now. I widen my eyes, but he doesn't react. He only concentrates on the job at hand.

It takes a minute to convince Polly this is really happening, and when the next contraction starts, he says, "Push, Polly. One... two... three..."

She props herself up and I try to hold her up, counting with her.

"Great, take a break, but we're going to go as soon as the next contraction starts. When I say now, push as hard as you can."

Polly nods.

"Now," he says.

She pushes.

"Harder, Polly, come on."

I can tell she's not giving it her all. "You have to get her out, which means you have to give it your all. Come on. Don't worry about anything else, just think of your baby. You got this."

The look of fear in her eyes tells me she's way too worried about shitting herself in front of a plane full of people. I would be too if a gorgeous man was between my legs as I delivered a baby.

"Forget it. All that matters is that baby."

Polly nods.

"Okay, let's go again," GI Joe says. "Now!"

"One... two... three," I count down for her.

"Great work. Give me one second, the head is out," he says.

I can't see what he's doing, but suddenly a shrill cry comes from the little one.

"Almost there. Give me one good push and let's see if that does it."

Polly gives it her all, her face bright red, sweat dripping down to her chest. Her knuckles are white, stopping all circulation in my hands.

"That's it," I encourage her.

A few minutes later, GI Joe places a crying baby on her chest. "Congratulations, it's a girl."

Polly holds her and I smile at them, lost in my thoughts until Gladys says, "It was just a little bit, Polly, no worries."

Chapter Five

T he plane lands at the nearest airport, which happens to be Minneapolis.

"Here you go, Tre." Angie hands me my soiled clothes in a white garbage bag. If it wasn't my fatigues, I would toss them.

"Thanks."

"I'm so sorry again." Polly is being loaded on the airplane wheelchair that barely fits through the aisles.

"Just worry about yourself and the baby," I tell her.

"I feel like I should go with you," the brunette—I've found out her name is Tessa—says.

"No. Go get your man. I've got my happiness, go get yours." Polly holds the baby lovingly.

"I'm going to go with her. Until we can get her reunited with her family." Gladys walks behind the medical team pushing the wheelchair.

"What about your son?" Tessa asks.

Women amaze me. They were all seated together for less than two hours, but they act as though they're long-lost best friends who see each other every week for book club. Two men could sit by one another and the only thing they'd find out is the other's favorite sports team.

"He can miss me for once. Wonder how I'm doing. As long as I get there before Christmas, it will be fine."

"Gladys, really, I'll be fine," Polly says.

I watch the young mother and worry for her. The look in her eyes reminds me of me after I joined the military at eighteen years old. After basic training, being shipped out and landing in a world so foreign from anything I knew. It's a hell of a shock.

"Nonsense. Oh." She pulls out a piece of paper. "Tessa dear, here's my number. I turn it off at night, but I wake up early." She hands it to her.

"And I friended you on Insta," Polly says as people clap as she leaves the plane.

I shake my head, but when I feel eyes on me, I turn to my right to find Tessa glaring. Of course. I don't think she has any other type of expression in her arsenal where I'm concerned.

"What?" I ask.

"You. What are you shaking your head for?"

"It's just... women," I say with a shrug.

She cocks her head in a way I'm becoming familiar with. I've seen it so much in our short time together. "Women? Did you have no women soldiers in your unit?"

"We had two of them."

"Them." She growls under her breath, "Men are so annoying." She stomps down the aisle.

"Yet you're following one across the country."

She turns back my way and you'd think we're in a showdown at the O.K. Corral. Does she think she can draw faster than me? No fucking way. I watch her chest rise and fall as her gorgeous blue eyes grow darker, more like the depths of the ocean now. Then she circles back around and leaves.

"Man, she really doesn't like you," a woman I don't know says and slides out to exit the plane.

Which has me wondering, why are they exiting the plane? I look around as people grab their bags and start to head back up to where my seat is.

The woman sitting next to me in first class sees me and smiles wide. "While we have the time, why don't you and me head to the lounge? I'm sure you could use a drink."

"I'm sorry. I assumed the flight would take off again now that Polly and the baby are off."

She laughs and paws at my arm, her long fake fingernails scraping my skin. Since I had to change my clothes, I'm in civilian clothes now. "Oh, you didn't hear? All the praise you were getting for delivering a baby, I'm not surprised. I guess since it's so late and there's a snow and windstorm expected to hit the area within the next ten minutes, they want us to wait it out until morning. Maybe you and I can find a hotel room to pass the time."

I'd say I'm surprised by how forthcoming she is, but I've seen worse. For some reason, once they find out you're a soldier, they have unrealistic expectations. We're not really human to them. We're these heroes they put on a pedestal, and once they see our faults, faults that normal people have, they're shocked for some reason.

"Are you serious? Morning?" My head rocks back.

As much as I'm always a little hesitant to return to my hometown, my mom will be upset if I don't get home.

"Afraid so." She reaches toward the overhead bin, but pretends she's incapable of retrieving her bag. "Could you?"

I grab her rolling carry-on from the overhead bin and drop it at her feet.

"So strong," she coos.

I need off this plane and I'm going to ask not to be seated

41

next to her on the trip to Portland. I politely decline her offer and explain that I'm in need of some rest.

Everyone files out of the plane. When I get inside the airport, I see it's desolate. Most of the gates are dark, there's no holiday music playing, the restaurants are closed. A few workers are picking up trash after a busy holiday travel day.

Most of the passengers find seats. Some parents are keeping kids who were sleeping busy. Many hold the smaller ones and rock side to side. A few couples are off to the side, fighting from the stress of the situation.

I sit down at a gate a good distance away and observe. If I ever have a family, which wouldn't be any day soon, what kind of dad would I be? Before going away, I would've thought fun-loving, but I hardly find excitement in anything anymore.

"All the fangirls getting to be too much for you?" Tessa says from somewhere near me, but I don't see her.

I swivel in my seat. Sure enough, there she is closer to the window, on the floor, stretching. Damn, she's flexible.

"My hand hurts from all the autographs. Need a break."

"Could get carpal tunnel, better be careful." She practically does the splits, opening her legs so wide, and moves to the left, then the right, to stretch out her ribcage.

"I didn't know you were here."

Her forehead crinkles. "Is that code for if you'd known you wouldn't have sat over here?"

"No, I just meant…"

"It's okay. The feeling is mutual." She rolls to her stomach and folds her body in half with her ass in the air as she walks her hands back, slowly standing.

Impressive, but I'd never tell her that.

"Any word on the plane?" I ask.

"From what I heard, we're here until morning. I'm not going to fight everyone and their mother for a hotel room around here that'll probably cost me triple what it's worth."

"So, you're sleeping at the airport?"

She looks around. "No." Our eyes meet, and she rolls hers. "I'm kidding. Yes, the airport. I wasn't going to build an igloo outside on the runway, as much as you probably wish I would."

"I'm not sure I remember wishing you bodily harm."

"Oh, I'm alone in that then?" She crinkles her eyes and I almost let myself laugh, but refrain.

I stand and hitch my bag over my shoulder. When I pull my cell phone out to message my family, I see that I have no signal. "Did you already call your family?"

"I would have if I had any." She continues to exercise.

I wish I could take my words back. She doesn't have any family?

"No signal." I hold up my phone.

"Will Mommy send out the FBI? Alert: Missing soldier. Last seen being a hero delivering a baby on a plane flying across the country." She imitates the voice of a reporter.

"How do you know *I* have family?"

She stops stretching and stares at me from between her legs. I have the willpower of a fucking saint for not staring at her ass. "You seem like the type."

"You have an awful lot of opinions on me when you don't actually know anything about me." I move away from her, about to leave. The thought of running into my first-class seat mate isn't high on my priority list though.

"What can I say? You're not the first of your kind I've met." She sits in a chair and brings her knees up, wrapping her arms around them.

"What did your psychic say about me? That you'll meet a devastatingly handsome man on your way to a douche?"

"Devastatingly handsome?" Her perfectly arched brows almost reach her hairline. "You have no idea if he's a douche."

I shrug my shoulder. "I think I do."

"And why would that be?"

"Forget I said anything. I'm outta here." I walk away before I get myself into more drama today.

How I know he's a douche though is because he let her slip through his fingers. Didn't know how good he had it. Not that I care, I don't want a relationship, but if I was looking for one, Tessa would be the kind of woman I was looking for. I like a woman with fire in her eyes who gives as good as she gets.

Once I've left her, I can finally breathe normally again. She drives me crazy. Unfortunately, I enjoy crazy. I enjoy the banter. Hell, I get off on the banter. But I'm going home for the holidays, not picking up some woman who's traveling across the country for some other guy anyway.

I go to the bathroom and clean the shit off my fatigues as best I can. I didn't even notice at first, too terrified about delivering a baby on a plane. A million things could've gone wrong, but as always, the adrenaline pushed all those fears away. I only thought of getting through the mission.

Heading back out of the bathroom, I notice that a lot of the families are gone—to a hotel or not, I don't know. The details on the board now says that the flight will take off at seven in the morning.

I assume my parents will get the update somehow, since I can't contact them.

There's a bin with pillows and blankets. Nothing that looks too comfortable unless you're a four-year-old child—or a soldier. I grab a pillow and a blanket and sit on the floor, leaning against a wall. I've slept in worse conditions, so this shouldn't be too bad.

My eyelids are slowly lowering when I hear a huge screech coming from the area Tessa was in. I jump up and bolt in that direction, telling the people I pass that I've got it, to just stay put.

She's up on a chair when I reach her, tucking her hair behind her ears and scouring the floor all around her.

"What is it?" I ask.

"Nothing. I'm fine."

I blow out a breath. "The sooner you tell me, the quicker we can be away from one another again."

She looks at me. "A cockroach went by."

"Aren't you from New York?"

Never in a million years did I think this woman would be scared of a cockroach.

"You think cockroaches are all over New York?"

"No. But it can't be the first one you've ever seen." I walk around, searching for the insect in question.

"Obviously not, but it is the first one that's scurried along my feet." She jumps from one seat to the other like a child playing hot lava.

"It's probably long gone now."

"You don't know that." She continues to hop along, investigating every inch of the floor.

"Trust me, they're more scared of you than you are of them."

Her hands fist and her face grows red. "Why does everyone say that? It's such bullshit! If that were true, you'd never even see them because they'd stay hidden."

I shrug. Can't really argue with her logic. "Then change where you're sleeping."

She looks around and her lips continue to pull down into a frown, which is going to make me do something I shouldn't bother doing.

"Here," I say and move a bunch of furniture together to make a makeshift bed for her.

"Cockroaches can jump." A full body shiver runs through her.

"Well, you're looking for a solution I can't give you."

"I know." She stands there, her gaze constantly roaming the floor. "I'm just not going to sleep."

I roll my eyes and tell her to stay put, then grab my stuff and head back over to her. "Here, I'll sleep with you. Now does that make it better?"

"I can kill the bug. I just need to find it."

"You might never see it again." I sit on one of the rows of seats, putting my feet up on the other side and using my pillow in the crook of my neck.

"You can just sleep like that?" She sits similar to me, but opposite.

"This is like the Four Seasons."

I hear her move around a little, but I don't open my eyes.

Eventually sleep must come because by the time I wake up the next morning, there's life again at the airport, but mostly angry people arguing with the airline employees, by the looks of it. Not a good sign.

I stand and look out the window. "Holy shit." There's so much snow whipping around.

I pack my bag and head over to where others are, but a man I recognize from our flight stops me first.

"Hey, if you want a rental car, you better get down there. I heard they're running out," he says.

"A rental car?"

He nods. "The airport's shut down. Huge storm came through while we were sleeping." He holds up a stuffed elephant. "Had to come back and get this, but we're going to drive the rest of the way because my wife is one of those people that just has to keep moving. But I'm not joking, the line was long. I wish I could sleep anywhere like you and her."

I follow the direction his finger is pointing and see Tessa curled up into a ball, clutching the blanket as if she was cold last night.

"Thanks. Safe travels," I tell him.

Fuck. I look at the ticket boards and see that everything says canceled.

The ticket agent gets on the intercom, probably tired of repeating the same thing to everyone in line. "Passengers set to leave on flight 1365 to Portland, I'm sorry, but the airport is closed due to high winds and the inability to keep the runway de-iced. Most of the planes that were due to come in last night were unable to do so. I don't have a crystal ball that will tell me when flights will be rescheduled, but you will all be going on standby. Which means you could be waiting days. If you have yet to secure lodging in the area, I would suggest you do so now."

Groans echo throughout the area. Couples look at one another, deciding on the best option for them. Maybe this is some sign to drive home. Give myself a little more time before I have to see my family. More time to prepare for their disappointment. I sure as hell don't want to hang out at an airport listening to Christmas music and eating crap food for days.

I grab my bag, take one look at Tessa, and walk away. She'll be fine. She can definitely handle herself. She doesn't need me —in fact, she'd probably resent me for trying to look out for her. Plus, if there are limited cars, I need to get one.

Chapter Six

TESSA

The feeling of someone tapping my shoulder jolts me awake and I stare into the eyes of an airline ticket agent. He smiles, showing off his perfectly white teeth. "Good morning. I just wanted you to know that all flights have been canceled, so you should probably decide what you're going to do."

I toss the blanket over me to the side and put my feet on the floor, looking around at a completely empty terminal. Outside the windows, it's pure white from snow being tossed around by the howling wind. "Canceled?"

He nods, offering his best sympathetic expression that I'm sure he's had to give plenty of times today. "Afraid so. Big storm came through. Heavy winds. No one predicted that it would be this bad. My assumption is the airport will be closed for at least today. Once things open up again, you'll be on standby, so if you stay, you're taking your chances. Now, you could check into a hotel and call the airline, but from what I'm hearing, you'll be on hold for some time, and they can't rebook flights before the airport reopens anyway."

"Oh." Panic starts to take hold, but I shove it down. "So,

what should I do?" I look around again. "Where did everyone go?"

"Some went to hotels, but a lot went to the rental car desks, deciding they might get there faster if they drove. I don't have to tell you how crazy it will be once this airport opens." He cringes and rears his head back. "Say a little prayer for me, will ya?"

I smile, but then realize if no one is up here, they're all downstairs. "Thanks." I collect all my belongings and offer him the blanket and pillow, but he waves me off.

"All yours."

"Thanks." I stuff them in my carry-on and wheel the suitcase down the terminal.

"UGGHHH," I groan to myself.

On the ride down the escalator to the baggage claim and rental car area, I see that it's more chaotic down here. People are scrambling, arguing about their bags and when they'll receive them. The weird thing is there are no lines for the rental car places. So I figure I'll get a car first and then my bag.

But my stomach sinks as I walk by the rental car places. They all have handwritten signs stating they're sold out.

Panic awakes again inside me, my heart hammering and my gut churning like a salad spinner. What if I can't get a car? Thankfully Andrew paid for my ticket, but I didn't plan on spending a lot of money on this trip. I closed my dream business only two weeks ago after putting every penny I had into it. I have a small inheritance from my great-uncle, but it's not much.

I rush toward the desk that still has one person behind the counter, helping a customer. I wait, taking in the chaotic scene until I face forward for longer than a second and realize the guy ahead of me is GI Joe. I hadn't recognized him from the back without his uniform on.

The rental car employee is typing, and she leans past him

and looks right at me. "Ma'am, I'm sorry, but this is my last car. Wanted to let you know so you can go to one of the other desks."

I turn and look down the long line of vacant car rental places. "You're the last one open."

She follows my vision and purses her lips, giving me her best sympathetic look. "I'm sorry. But this is my last one."

GI Joe decides to turn around at the exact moment tears pool in my eyes. "Hey, Sleeping Beauty. Didn't dream about any cockroaches slipping into your mouth, did you?"

The tears retract in my eyes as if they were never there. "No, because it's climbing up your leg right now."

Even the woman behind the counter raises on her tiptoes and looks on as our fearless soldier jumps and shakes out his jeans. I giggle, and I catch the woman trying to stifle her laugh as she buries her head in the computer.

"I just need your license and credit card," she says to him.

He pulls out his identification and credit card and places them on the counter.

"What if I pay double?" I ask, surprising myself, stepping up to the counter next to him. How can a man smell this good after spending the night in an airport?

"Oh no. I can't do that," she says.

He turns to me. "You can step back now."

"Oh dear," she says, staring at his license, his credit card left on the counter.

Hope flickers to life inside me.

"Is there a problem?" he asks, clearly not thinking there is. As if she's saying oh dear because his driver's license picture is so amazing, she can't stop looking it. Yeah, right.

Her gaze rises from the license to him and it's clear she's a people pleaser because she's fighting with herself to tell him. "It's expired." She bites her lip as though it took all her willpower to get that out.

"No, it's not."

She holds it out and he takes it, scouring it. When his shoulders fall, that tiny spark of hope bursts into a flame.

"I have a license!" I raise my hand and open my purse to grab it.

"It must have expired while I was out of the country. What about my military license? The US Government trusts me to drive Humvees. They cost an ungodly amount, surely I can drive your car."

"I can't release a car without a valid driver's license," she says with regret.

I continue to dig through my purse, wondering what I could've done with it. The slower I am to find it, the more time he has to convince her.

"She can't even find hers. Look how disorganized she is. And you'll trust her just because hers didn't expire two months ago?"

I look at him through my eyelashes, offended, although seriously, where the hell is my license? "First off, I live in New York City, okay? I don't need it on a daily basis." Then I feel a hard rectangle card and hold it up as though I won Bingo. "Here it is!"

I slap it on the desk and give him a smug smile.

She picks it up and studies it. "I'll need a credit card too."

I slide closer, moving GI Joe out of the way, and he grumbles something I can't hear.

"That should only take her about another twenty minutes to locate." He stuffs his hands into his pockets.

"That's where you're wrong because I use my credit card a lot more often." I pick it out of my purse and hold it in the air. "See? You can shoo now because the last car is mine."

I place the card on the counter and slide his credit card to the edge of the counter toward him, unable to read anything other than that Abner is his first name. Poor guy. Good thing he's hot. He's got that going for him.

For some reason, he doesn't pick up his bag and leave. I turn my back and start to fill out the paperwork.

"Why don't you guys travel together? You could share gas or something," she says, inputting my information into the computer.

"No," we say in unison.

"Oh dear," she says again just as she did earlier, and the pen I'm holding stills.

"What is it?" GI Joe raises up on his toes to see what the problem is, but I raise on my tiptoes, trying to block his view.

She stares at me for a moment. "Your credit card has been declined."

My stomach sinks. How is that possible? And then I remember that before I went to see the psychic, I splurged on that designer dress. My last "feel sorry for myself" shopping trip. Shit.

"I have another one!" I raise my finger and dig through my purse again.

They both blow out a breath.

"I can pay for the car, she can't. Isn't that more important? I swear I'll go the speed limit and drive responsibly. You can trust me." He continues trying to convince her, and the way she hems and haws makes me feel as if she might just agree.

"Here you go." I pull my great-uncle's wallet from my purse and put his credit card on the counter.

GI Joe stares down with crinkles in his forehead. "She's trying to use her boyfriend's card. How do you know she didn't steal that wallet?"

"I didn't steal it. It's my dead uncle's."

The card slips from the woman's hand and falls to the floor. "Ma'am, I cannot use a card you're not authorized to use."

53

I whip my head in his direction and narrow my eyes. "She wouldn't have noticed, thanks for that."

He grins at me. "You're welcome."

Right then, a man comes up behind us. "Tell me you have another car," he says with desperation coating his features.

"Well..." The woman looks between us.

"No. She only has one left and it's mine," I say.

He must sense something is off because he steps up next to me and looks between GI Joe and me. "I'll pay triple."

"No. It doesn't work like that," I say.

"I'm not talking to you," he says with a scowl.

You can tell he's a businessman. Three-piece suit, a little wrinkled from wherever he slept or didn't sleep last night. His hair is a little messy, but he's clean-shaven, which makes no sense. He pulls out a black Amex card, flashing it in front of us all. "Please, I need to get home."

"So do the rest of us," GI Joe says.

The woman looks at us, handing us back our cards. "I have no choice. If you're not traveling together, with your driver's license"—she turns to me and then to him—"and your credit card, then I have to give the car to this gentleman."

Knowing this is just a shit show waiting to happen, I look at GI Joe with raised eyebrows.

He rocks back on his heels. "What? We'll kill one another."

"We don't really have a choice." I absolutely hate the fact that I need him.

He looks at the man who's already trying to sweet-talk the woman.

"It's ours. I'll pay for it." The soldier slides his credit card over to her.

"I hope it goes through," I say.

"It will."

And it does. She holds up the keys for me since it's my

driver's license on file. "Enjoy your trip, you two. I hope I don't see you on the news." She smiles sweetly, and I snag the keys out of her hand.

We grab our bags from the carousel and head in the direction of the car lot she gave us.

The man from the counter follows us. "I have about three grand on me. I'll give it all to you if you just give me the car."

I stop and look at GI Joe. Three grand sounds nice. Fifteen hundred between us.

But when neither of us budge, the businessman becomes more persistent. "How about I give you my credit card to use however you can to get home, plus the three grand? That's all I've got on me."

He's sweating around his temples. The desperation practically oozes from his pores.

"It's the holidays, sure, but why are you so desperate to get home?" GI Joe asks him.

He blows out a breath and runs a hand through his hair. "My wife will kill me. She doesn't even know I'm here. She thought I was in LA, spending the night before flying back to San Francisco to our family."

"But you were..." I arch an eyebrow.

He studies me for a moment but shifts to GI Joe, lowering his voice, "With another woman."

"Yeah, no can do," I say and turn around.

"Please," he begs from behind me.

GI Joe stands between us, so I stop at the sliding doors and ask him, "Who are you with?"

"You. Definitely you." GI Joe follows me to the shuttle outside.

We have to brace ourselves against the snow whipping around and the freezing temperatures. This drive is not going to be a cakewalk.

On the shuttle, I sit down. "Why are men such assholes?" I shake my head, talking more to myself than him.

"We're not all assholes." He takes a seat a few down from me.

"You were about to take his side, bail him out."

He guffaws. "No, I wasn't."

"Then why would you stand there like that?"

He shakes his head. "No reason."

"Because you felt bad for the guy. All of you stick together. It's pathetic."

He doesn't say anything, and the shuttle drops us off at the car that looks almost matchbox size. We'll be lucky if our luggage fits in the trunk.

After thanking the shuttle driver, I open up the car and put my suitcase in before heading to the driver's side.

"You're going to drive?" he asks.

"Well, I am the one with the legal driver's license."

"Yeah, but the weather. Have you driven in snow before?"

"Stop being a sexist pig and get in the passenger seat."

I crawl into the car, and man, it's small. Like his muscular arm is touching my small arm. The entire small interior fills with his manly scent immediately. Is that an army thing? Do they spray them with pheromones to help them seduce the enemy?

"How many hours to Portland?" I ask, wondering how I'm going to be able to handle being so closely confined with a man who equal parts drives me insane and makes me want to jump his body.

"About twenty-seven hours."

My eyes widen. Shit. Which one of us didn't think this through?

"We can drive through the night and be there by tomorrow morning depending on the roads. But you'd have to let me drive."

"We'll see. Sit tight, Rambo, someone else is in the driver's seat now."

I start the car and it sounds as if it took a hamster running on a wheel to get going.

Oh, Carter, you better be worth this.

Chapter Seven

TRE

My eyes flutter open to "Extraordinary Merry Christmas" playing on the radio. It takes me a moment to take in my surroundings before I remember I'm in the passenger seat of the world's smallest car with a woman who hates me behind the wheel. I rub my eyes and look at Tessa. She's dancing in her seat, singing while her fingers tap to the beat on the steering wheel. Her cheeks are rosy from the heat blasting at our faces from the vent.

I look out the frosted windows at the endless snow stretching as far as I can see, whipping up off the snowbanks on the sides of the road. Her apparent ease at navigating the snow-slick roads might comfort some, but I see it as a sign that she's not navigating them with the care she should.

"Where are we?" I crack my neck, moving my hand to the heater controls.

Smack.

I retract the hand Tessa just slapped and stare at her.

"It's important for the driver to be comfortable, and I run cold." She smiles not-so-sweetly at me before looking back at the road, thank God.

"I run hot."

She looks at me and shrugs. "Driver's rules rule."

"Fine, pull over, and I'll drive." I reach over again and turn down the heat, only for her to immediately turn it back up an extra degree just to be difficult. I don't know why I'm surprised.

"No worries, because we'll be stopping in a little bit." Her impish grin says she's up to something I'm probably not going to like.

"For gas?" I peer over, but we still have a little less than half a tank.

"Nope."

"Food? I could eat." My stomach growls as if to agree.

"Nope." She pops the 'p' in the word.

"Mind clueing me in?" I point at the map on her phone that's displaying the GPS. "Because it looks like we're supposed to be on this road over here and now we're on this one." My finger is on a line that's moving away from the one we should be on.

"There was a sign on the side of the highway and my gut said to go check it out, so I turned off the highway."

I draw in a deep breath for patience. "And you didn't think to consult me?"

I cannot believe she's going to take us however many miles off course because her gut told her to. Instead of getting angry, I try to rein myself in because she has the valid license, which means I need her.

"You were sleeping. By the way, you snore." She sways right and left to the music.

My face screws up. "I do not snore."

"Okay," she says in a singsong voice.

"I'm pretty sure my team would have told me if I snore. We don't keep things like that from one another. They'd be busting my balls about it."

She shrugs. "Okay then. I guess there's a dog in the car." She looks behind us and lifts her eyebrows at me.

"I'm not joking. I don't snore."

"Okay." She turns on her turn signal and stops at the light.

"So, where are we going?" I ask for what feels like the millionth time. How the hell will I get through the next day traveling with her? Did I say I like crazy? Hopefully she falls asleep once I start driving.

"The World's Largest Gingerbread House!" She turns to me with an expectant look, as if I should be as excited as her.

"That's what the detour is for?" I deadpan.

"There were all these signs teasing it on the highway. Like how much candy they used to build it. It's twenty-two feet tall, can you believe that?"

"My life is complete. I can't imagine if I died before seeing it." I press my forehead to the cold window.

"Fine, be sarcastic." She clearly hears the edge in my voice. "You're not going to dampen my excitement."

"I'll just stay in the car."

"Then you're going to be cold."

"You won't leave the keys for me?" After thinking about it for a second, I can see why she wouldn't.

"And come out, and you're gone? I'm not naive, as much as you probably think I am."

"I don't think you're naive. I think you lack organization and a plan. Like we're driving straight to Portland, but we're not in the car a couple hours and we're headed off course to see an oversized gingerbread house."

She flips on her turn signal when the sign for the gingerbread house comes into view.

"What a waste of someone's time," I mumble as she drives down a gravel driveway covered in snow and ice.

She turns off the car and sits with the keys in her hand, her jaw hanging open, staring at me.

"What?" I ask.

"Who are you to judge how someone should spend their time? Look around. All kinds of people are here to see it. They've decided not to follow the traditional path, but follow one filled with laughter and spontaneity, making memories they'll always have. Live a little, GI Joe. I'm sure even you deserve it."

She gets out of the car and puts on the coat she took off to drive. I want to be angry, demand that we stay on track. At this rate, I won't make it home before Christmas—which reminds me, I need to text my family.

I get out and soak her in across the roof of the car, her eyes sparkling with anticipation as she continues to hum Christmas songs. I don't have it in me to take this away from her.

"Fine, but an hour max." I lift my watch and set the timer.

"Ten-four." She salutes me.

I inhale a deep, calming breath, following her up the steps. Maybe someone can poke me in the eye with a candy cane while I'm here.

We walk up the wooden stairs that are a lawsuit waiting to happen.

"Name is Tre, by the way," I offer, realizing we haven't exchanged formal introductions.

"Tre?"

"Yep."

"Huh, I thought it was Abner." A smile tips the edges of her lips.

Fucking hell. "Abner is a family name. I'm a third, so they call me Tre."

"Because you don't want to be called Abner? You could have gone Ab? Or Ab-man, Ab-dawg, Ab-ster? There are surprisingly a lot of options." She stops where we have to buy the tickets to see the giant gingerbread house, because of course it isn't free. "And since you didn't want to come here,

I'll pay for your ticket, which is just a donation." She points to where it says donations help with the upkeep throughout the season.

I don't argue as she pulls out her great-uncle's wallet and takes out a ten, paying for us both.

"I'm Tessa," she says, putting out her hand.

"I know. I heard Gladys and Polly calling you that."

"Good, then no GI Joe and no princess." She raises her finger. "Permission to call you Abner, sir," she says with a mock salute.

"Permission denied."

"Just so you know"—she leans in close, the light scent of her perfume that must be two days old at this point, but still makes my dick twitch in my pants, wafting over me—"I'm an 'ask for forgiveness rather than permission' kinda gal. I was just trying to be nice." She walks off to go look at the ginger-bread house.

The wind whips the snow around outside, but I think it's actually too cold to snow at this point. Thankfully, they have little heaters around. There are booths set up that sell home-made cookies, donuts, and hot chocolate, along with a knick-knack shop with ornaments and signs you can purchase that brag that you've visited the world's largest gingerbread house.

I'll never admit it to Tessa, but the house is kind of cool. It has multiple rooms, fully furnished with extravagant facades made of gingerbread and colorful candies.

My mom would love this place. She'd love Tessa and the fact she had to stop to see it. I watch her from a good distance as she talks with a family who have younger kids with them. They discuss how unique this place is, how over the top and how it makes her want to build one herself.

She's pulled her long dark hair under a knit hat with a pom-pom on top, the exposed dark locks framing her face. Her rosy cheeks are the only color on her pale face. Her snugly fitting red coat is bright against the gray sky and snow-covered ground. But it's her smile as she talks to the family that warms me.

Her eyes sparkle with joy and I'm glad I didn't put up a bigger fight about not stopping here. I can't imagine if I would've taken this moment from her.

I stop and buy us each a hot chocolate, then find her searching the area for me. I break the distance, leaning in close to her once I'm near. "Miss me?"

She startles, one hand flying up under a cup of hot chocolate and launching it in the air. We both watch it flip over and fall to its death on the gravel path.

"Whoops," she says. "You scared me."

"I didn't know you were going to karate chop me." I hold out the other cup. "Here."

"Oh, I couldn't," she says, but her tongue licks her plump lips.

I've never wanted to be a cup of hot chocolate so badly in my life. "I'll go buy another one."

I leave it with her and head back to the booth, returning a few minutes later. She's intently watching a woman sitting in a rocking chair reading *How The Grinch Stole Christmas* to kids sitting on logs set out like seats.

Instead of scaring her this time, I stand at her side until she notices me.

"She does all these voices," she says in a quiet voice, enamored like a child.

"I see that."

Venturing off to admire the craftsmanship of the gingerbread house, it gets me thinking about my youth. She joins me after a minute at the fenced-off area.

"When I was younger, we had these gingerbread competitions," I say. "My mom would spend all day baking the gingerbread, and me, my brother, and sister would all get the pieces, frosting them to put it together. Then she'd fill bowls with candy so we could decorate."

She listens intently. I'm not even sure why I'm telling her this.

"Anyway, she'd always have the rest of the family on Christmas Eve be the judges, and whoever won got a little something extra in their stocking."

"That's a great tradition," she says.

"Yeah, my first year away from home, she sent me a kit. You know those boxes that are supposed to come with everything? I made it with my team, but it wasn't the same." I sip my hot chocolate, remembering how homesick I was.

"Those are nice memories." Her voice is soft and somewhat wistful.

I turn to her. "What about you? Wanting to come here, you must have memories of your own about building a gingerbread house?"

She shakes her head. "No."

There's a finality to her one word, so I let it go.

"I'll throw these out and we can go," she says, taking my hot chocolate before it's done.

As she walks away, I pull out my phone and pull up the family group chat.

> Me: Flight had an emergency landing, airport closed, rented a car to drive. Sorry, my signal has been spotty.

I glance at the bars and see I've got three now.

Lil'Bro: Mom already reported you missing. The search party didn't find you.

Lil'Sis: They told us at the airport. Be careful driving.

Dad: Remember, bridges are icy, and stop for gas before you hit a quarter tank, you can never be sure in the cold. You got this, son.

Mom: Oh, I wish you were home but you know what you're doing. Be safe, son. I love you.

Me: Thanks. We're going to try to drive the whole night through and be there late tomorrow.

Mom: We?

Lil'Sis: Who are you with?

Lil'Bro: Are you bringing a woman to Christmas?

Dad: Anyone is welcome to come.

Me: If you stop texting I can answer you. I'm traveling with someone, but it's a long story and I'll explain it when I get there. AND she will not be coming to Christmas. See you soon.

They each say goodbye and don't question me further about Tessa.

"Ready?" she asks.

I hold out my hand. "I'll drive the next leg."

"Don't get pulled over," she warns, passing the keys over.

"Trust me."

She rolls her eyes. "Famous last words."

We descend down the stairs, and as I watch her walk ahead of me, I can't shake the feeling that people have let her down a lot in her life. But that's not any of my concern.

"First stop will be food and rules," I say.

She stands by the passenger side of the car and looks at me as I make my way around to the driver's side. "Food and rules?"

I look over at the gingerbread house. "We can't be taking these little detours if we're going to get to Portland. It negates the whole reason for driving."

She stares at me over the roof of the car as though I'm the Grinch.

"Get in the car, Tessa." When she doesn't, I add, "I'm only stopping because I'm hungry. We need to eat."

She shakes her head and rolls her eyes—again.

Whatever. I just need her to understand that from here on out, there are no more little excursions.

Chapter Eight

Instead of getting back on the highway, Tre drives down the snow-filled streets of the small downtown area of whatever town we're in. It's typical of what I'd expect to find in a small town—specialty shops, a bakery, hardware store, butcher, some restaurants and bars. But tucked away on a side street sits a diner adorned with twinkling white lights and boughs of garland wrapped around the windows.

Tre parallel parks along the curb with zero effort. I try to tell myself that it's not sexy at all, but I'm impressed because it would probably have taken me five tries.

Inside the diner, the scent of coffee brewing mingles with the sweetness of cinnamon rolls that are proudly displayed beside a sign that says, "Best Cinnamon Rolls in five counties."

Holiday music floats from small speakers mounted on the walls, and every table has a mini artificial tree that's been decorated. The waitress wearing reindeer antlers escorts us to a red vinyl booth, past the line of stools that face the counter, where a group of men talk with each other.

I slide into one side of the booth and Tre does the same on

the other. We both turn our cups right side up on the paper doilies set on the table.

I slide my menu over to the edge of the table. "I already know what I'm getting."

"Have you been here before?" His eyebrows draw down, and he peers over his menu with those blue eyes of his. I'd have to be blind not to notice what a beautiful color they are, lined with thick eyelashes.

"No. But the smell alone and the sign were enough to decide. Cinnamon roll."

A waitress wearing a Santa hat comes over and pours us some coffee, eyeing Tre a little longer than necessary.

"You're going to eat a bowl of sugar for lunch?" he asks with judgment.

He never seems to notice when women are enamored by him. I only met the man less than twenty-four hours ago and I need two hands to count how many women are using him in their imaginations late at night in bed.

"No, I'm having a cinnamon roll," I clarify, pouring cream into my coffee, then adding a sugar packet.

"Which is essentially a bowl of sugar."

I blow out a breath and stare outside at a few kids running by with sleds. "Why don't you let me worry about what I'm consuming, and you worry about yourself?"

He lays down his menu. "It actually is my business. Consuming a lot of sugar can make you crash, and if you're driving and I fall asleep, I don't want to put my life in danger."

I stare at him with a blank expression. "Are you serious?"

He shrugs one strong shoulder. "I'm just saying."

"I'll have you know sugar fuels me for most of my day." I purposely take another sugar packet for my coffee even though I usually only take one sugar.

He watches me until I take the spoon out from stirring

and place it on the napkin. "Making a point?" He arches an eyebrow.

"And what are you having? Actually, let me guess." I pick up the menu and peruse it. "Obviously eggs, maybe just egg whites?" He shows no sign that I might be right. "Ham instead of sausage or bacon? And..." I read what else they offer. "I bet you're feta cheese over cheddar, or is all cheese considered bad for you? Tell me I'm wrong." I place the menu back down on top of the other one.

"I guess you'll have to wait to find out." He sips his black coffee.

The server with the reindeer antlers approaches our table for our order.

I order my cinnamon roll with a side of two scrambled eggs with cheddar cheese, purposely staring at Tre.

He shows no emotion on his face or in his eyes. I wish I was able to hide how much he's getting under my skin.

"I'll have an egg white omelet with bacon, onion, mush-rooms, and American cheese. Can I have an English muffin and fruit instead of hash browns?"

Zaryn, as her name tag says, picks up the menus, thanks us, and walks away.

"Way to splurge on the cheese. Did you decide on that just to prove a point to me?" I can't help the smile that slips free.

He takes his silverware out of the paper ring and puts the paper napkin in his lap as if the food is going to come immedi-ately. "I hate to disappoint you, but my decisions don't have anything to do with you."

I'd balk, but I feel my cheeks grow pink with embarrass-ment that he's not playing along with our banter, so I straighten my back against the booth and stare out the window.

We're both silent for a few minutes, and my mind wanders

to Carter and what I might expect when I reach him. What will his reaction be when I show up at his doorstep?

Maybe our breakup was mutual. He didn't fight me when I told him I wanted to call it quits, citing that we were just too busy. I was striving to make my bakery a success, and he was making a name for himself in IT. If we really wanted it to go somewhere, I could've not gone to bed so early, and maybe he could've stopped by the bakery in the morning. I'm sure he'll be surprised, especially since we never got to the serious part of our relationship, but something in my gut says I'm heading in the right direction by going to Portland.

"Listen, we should set some rules down before we embark on the rest of this trip." Tre's voice interrupts my thoughts.

"What kind of rules?"

"The kind that doesn't include gingerbread houses."

I huff. "You've been gone a long time, right? Don't you want to live a little? Not live by such a rigid schedule when you're not working?"

"I need to get back to my family."

"I understand that, but Christmas isn't for another week. We have time to get there."

"Tell that to my mom." He sips his coffee, diverting his gaze.

"Fine, I won't make any more impromptu stops." The only reason I'm agreeing is because he's making me feel guilty. Of course he wants to be with his family—who knows how long he's been gone? I would want to be with my family too, if I had one.

"Great. And as a thank you, I'll cover expenses."

"What?" My voice sounds a little screechy.

"You don't have a working credit card." He looks up at me through his eyelashes with an expression that says I can't argue that fact.

"I have my great-uncle's." It might not be mine, but he

wouldn't care that I'm using it. I plan on paying it back as soon as I find my footing.

"They will cancel it, you know that, right?"

Wouldn't I, as next of kin, have to cancel it?

"The funeral home will put his information into a system, and that cancels all open credit by stating he's deceased." He's talking to me as if I'm stupid.

It only reminds me of my uncle. Always lecturing me on how I have no idea what the real world is like, but never realizing I knew exactly how heartless some people could be. Including him. I was raised without anyone truly loving me until Kenzie came along.

"How do you know that?"

He raises his eyebrows and I instantly feel bad for asking. He's probably seen a lot of death, some maybe his close friends.

"I didn't know that. Well, I have some cash," I say.

"I'm happy to cover you. My mom would probably kill me if I didn't."

My fingers twist in my lap. "I can't pay you back anytime soon." Embarrassment coats me like a paint can tipping over my head.

"It's okay."

"No. I'm serious. I just lost the bakery I had in New York, and I literally have nothing to my name." I frown.

"And yet you're traveling across the country to find love?" He asks the question as though I'm stupid, and irritation jolts inside me like a lightning bolt.

"'Tis the season to find love. Christmas miracles and all that."

His lips tip up just a bit, and I have the thought that I'd give anything to see what he looks like when he smiles fully.

"What?" I ask.

"Your Christmas miracle is to find the one who got away?"

I sip my coffee. "You make it sound so stupid."

"No." He shakes his head and lifts his coffee mug, gesturing for me to tap mine to his, just as our food arrives. "To Christmas miracles. I don't understand it, but I hope you get one."

We eat in mostly silence, and I keep all the questions I have for him to myself. He doesn't seem like someone who wants to share.

He pays the bill, and I make note of the amount in my notes app on my phone so I can add up what I'll owe him at the end of this trip. Hopefully it won't be too much money.

"So, was it the best cinnamon roll?" he asks as we leave and zip up our coats before venturing to the car.

"I'd have to taste the ones in the other five counties," I say.

"Well, that's for another time."

I follow him to the car. Once I reach the passenger door, I take off my jacket and throw it in the back, shivering when the wind hits me.

"Actually." I look back at the diner. "If I'm being completely honest with you, I think I bake a better one."

He rocks his head back and looks at me over the hood of the car. "So, your decision to eat a bowl of sugar was all about ego?"

"What can I say? I had to see." I shrug then rub my hands together.

"Well, I fucking love that you did that, especially that you're honest enough with yourself to admit yours is better." He opens his door and folds himself into the car.

I stand outside for another second because I think he just complimented me. His words shouldn't have made me feel all warm and cozy inside, but they did anyway.

Damn him.

Chapter Nine

TESSA

"If you're so cold, you need to put your coat on," he says, turning down the heat again.

"See the snow outside, the frost on the windows... it's winter, which means it's cold as fuck out there, and we're in a tin can for a car." I turn the knob to crank the heat up again.

"I'm the driver, so I'm in control, remember? I'm not the one who made that rule." He raises both eyebrows at me.

God, he loves to challenge everything. Just when I was starting to like him for more than his looks.

"I understand that I made that rule, but you're being unrealistic." I unbuckle my seat belt and turn around to grab my jacket.

"What are you doing?" he shouts. "You can't unbuckle your seat belt when we're in a moving vehicle on roads as shitty as these."

"I'm getting my jacket to lay over me, and FYI, I'm taking yours too."

"Fine, if it stops you from blasting the heat like we're in a tent at the North Pole."

I sit back down in my seat, buckling myself up. When it clicks, I give him a look to ask if he's happy now. Then I cover my legs with my jacket and use his jacket over my torso.

"Now we're both happy," he says, turning down the heat. "Why don't you take a little nap?"

I narrow my eyes at him. "I'm not a child who needs to be put down for a nap."

"I could argue that you act like one."

I squeeze my eyes shut. *Don't let him bait you, Tess.*

"There you go. Night. Night." He presses a button on the radio, so it plays country music.

Not wanting to listen to endless songs about heartbreak, I turn my body to face the window and close my eyes.

He lightly hums to himself, and for whatever reason, the sound is somewhat soothing. The scent of him has soaked into his jacket and it wraps around me like a soft blanket, causing my eyes to grow heavy. Pretty soon, I lose the battle against sleep.

I'm not sure how long I sleep for, but when I wake, the car isn't moving. I pry one eye open to notice it's dark outside, then the entire car shakes. I startle and tear the coats off to see a semi-truck's taillights flying down the highway. We must be parked on the side of the road.

The driver's seat is vacant, but the car is still running.

The hair on the back of my neck stands on end. This feels like one of those movies where the man just leaves. Or maybe we got pulled over?

Nope, there're no flashing police lights behind us.

Where is Tre? He wouldn't leave me here all by myself. Then again, what do I really know about him? I dig through my purse and find a pen is my only weapon at hand. That won't do shit if someone tries to come at me.

My side of the window is fogged up. When I open the

76

door, it hits something, and I have to push harder to get the door to swing all the way open.

"What the fuck?" I hear Tre shout, but then there's kind of an echo and another semi-truck passes us. The wind barrels around me like a tornado.

"Tre?" I call into the dark night.

"Down here."

I can't see anything, so I grab my cell phone from the car and turn on the flashlight, shining down the bank of snow. "Tre?"

All I hear is a groan. I take a few steps, but it's icy, the snow hardening under the frigid temperatures. Finally, I spot Tre lying on the snow with his back facing me, his bare ass hanging out of his pants.

Man, Polly was right. It really is a nice ass.

"What are you doing down there?"

"I just decided to take a nap, Tessa. What do you think? You hit me with the door and sent me flying down here."

I bite my lip at the anger in his voice before my defensiveness comes out to play. "Well, what were you doing out here to begin with?"

"I was taking a fucking piss," he yells, and his voice echoes in the cold night air.

I look around the pitch darkness of the unlit highway. There isn't anything or anyone around. "Why would you do it right by my door?"

"Take the flashlight off me so I can pull up my damn pants."

I move the flashlight away and have to remind myself that it's for the best that I won't get a glimpse of *all* of him. I don't need that visual running through my mind the entire time we're in the car together.

Then I hear the crunching of the snow from his boots

breaking the thin layer of hard frost. "Damn it all to hell. My pants are soaked now, and I'm bleeding."

"Bleeding?"

"Nothing I can't handle."

He finally reaches the car again, and he looks as if I ran him over. There are sporadic wet marks on his shirt and pants, his hair is in all different directions, and the skin on his face is cold and red.

I glance down to where blood drips off his forearm, making a red polka dot pattern in the snow. "We need to get you to the hospital."

"No, we don't. I just need a first aid kit." He disregards the cut that's still oozing blood and opens the back of the car, digging through the back.

"I doubt we have a first aid kit unless you travel with one." I follow him, bracing myself when another truck approaches. "We need to get off this road. It's dangerous."

"This is nothing," he grumbles.

"I'm taking over driving and we're getting you to a hospital."

"I'm not going to a hospital." He takes a T-shirt out of his bag and wraps it around his arm, pulling the fabric with his teeth to get it tight.

"I know I'm not a medic and can't deliver a baby on a plane or anything, but I can help you apply pressure if you want."

"I'm used to handling things on my own," he says, holding his arm with his other hand.

God, this man is so damn stubborn.

"I'm taking charge now." I round the back of the car, glance behind me, then plaster myself to the side of the car while another semi-truck barrels past me. I swear I almost blow away. Hell, the car and I could go with one good gust.

I hurriedly get in the driver's seat and put on my seat belt, waiting for him. He opens the door and slides into the seat beside me, then he tries to keep pressure on the cut and get his seat belt on at the same time.

"Here, let me." I unbuckle my seat belt.

"I've got it."

"Why do you have to be such a hardass?" I grab the metal part of his seat belt. I'm pulling it across him when I glance up for a second and lock eyes with him.

He blinks, and our shared moment ends. That was weird.

Then he says in a quiet voice, "I'm not used to relying on a lot of people, okay?"

I ignore that there's no apology in that statement for his snippiness. "Don't all soldiers rely on each other?"

He doesn't say anything for a while. "Out there, yes. But here, I'm the trained one."

"Stop being such a macho guy. I promise not to tell anyone I put on your seat belt."

He chuckles, and I glance up at him again before I click the seat belt in place. *Holy shit.* The seat belt slips from my hand, but I catch it before it gets all the way across his lap.

He's ten times more gorgeous when he smiles. I can see now how he got the first-class ticket. Even the small scar just above his right eyebrow makes him sexier somehow. Rugged and manly.

"What?" He stops chuckling and his face grows serious once more.

"You laughed," I admit. "And smiled."

His forehead wrinkles. This is closer to the expression I'm used to from him. "You act like I don't do that."

"Not with me, you haven't."

We're inches away from one another and my lips tingle with the need to place them on his.

"Congratulations, I'm human."

My laugh bubbles up out of me because that's not what I

expected him to say. "I wouldn't go that far." I take a glimpse and his T-shirt is almost soaked through where the cut is. "All right, tough guy, I'm taking you to the hospital."

He groans but doesn't argue, which makes me feel that more confident in my decision.

* * *

I get off the highway, following the GPS to what they say is the nearest hospital. Since Tre insists that he can walk, I drive past the emergency roundabout and park in the lot so we can both walk in.

Christmas music blares once we're inside. Doctors and nurses are dancing or talking around a spread of food and drinks in the lobby area. The sliding doors close behind us, and they all turn in our direction.

"Great. I'm sure this is better than if I stitched myself up. A drunk doctor doing it," Tre mumbles.

"I'm sure they're just drinking punch. Nothing wrong with getting in the holiday spirit." I elbow him in the ribs and approach the check-in desk after the woman in a light-up rein-deer sweater sits down behind the desk.

"He cut himself," I say.

"I didn't cut myself. Someone pushed me down a bank on the side of the road and a tree limb or something cut me."

"Semantics." I lean forward to the woman, pointing at the computer. "You might want to put in there that he's a difficult patient. He's military and wanted to do it himself."

The woman's eyes fog over with unshed tears. "Military? Which branch?"

"Army, ma'am."

"My son is a Marine. Are you from around here?"

The emotion on this woman's face is like a punch to the gut. She looks moments away from crying.

"No. We're headed back to Portland," Tre says.

"Going home to your parents?" she asks.

"Yes, ma'am."

"This is our first without him. Couldn't get leave."

Tre's lips purse and he nods. "First one is the hardest, for sure."

She wipes her tears. "Definitely." She wipes her face again and smiles. "Anywho, let's get you checked in, shall we?"

I turn away for a moment, pretending to give them their privacy and sit down to read a magazine. No one has ever missed me like that. That emptiness I've felt so often in my life from not having a family rises up, and fear grips me—what if Carter shuts the door in my face, and I'm left traveling back to New York alone on what could be Christmas? I rush into the bathroom and kneel in the stall, throwing up my entire cinnamon roll lunch.

There's a knock on the door. "Tessa?" Tre asks.

"I'll be right out." I flush the toilet once more, stand, and wash my hands, splashing water on my face. Once I look halfway presentable, I open the door to find Tre leaning on the other side of the wall.

"You okay?" he asks.

"Yeah. Just had to use the bathroom."

He studies me for a long while, and I shift my feet, staring down at them. "Speaking of, I need you to help me go to the bathroom."

My head flies up. "What?"

"Yeah, undo my pants and pull it out. Maybe hold my dick to aim it in the toilet."

"You can't be serious."

He laughs again, this one heartier and louder than the one in the car. "Is that a no?"

I can't help but smile at him, despite my mood a moment ago. "I thought you didn't need anyone's help?"

"Tre, I have a room for you," the woman from the check-in desk says, interrupting us.

"Saved by Mags." He winks and walks back her way.

I follow with a smile. I can't help but think he knows that I wasn't just going to the bathroom. How on earth can a soldier read people so well? Maybe Tre isn't who I've pinned him to be.

Chapter Ten

W e're placed in an exam room, and I'm told to take off my shirt and put on a gown.

"If you'd like me to leave..." Tessa shifts her weight from the chair to stand.

"That's okay. I'm sure you've seen a man's chest before."

"I'm happy to just wait outside the whole time."

"That's okay. I might need a witness if they cut off my arm or something." I grab the hem of my shirt and slowly raise it up my torso.

She lowers back down into the chair, her eyes remaining on me until I clear my throat.

"Sorry, I zoned out." She turns her head so fast I worry she strained something.

I finish taking off my shirt and put it on the other empty chair. I glance at the gown and put it on so the ties are at my back.

"Do you mind tying me in the back? Don't want to give away a free show."

She laughs. I'd never tell her this, but I haven't heard

anything so beautiful in years. Maybe it's my ego because she's laughing at something I said.

I offer her my back and her fingers scrape my bare skin while grasping the tie strings.

"Sorry," she whispers.

I close my eyes, feeling her breath brush my neck and making the little hairs stand on end. Her touch is gentle, and I have to stop myself from leaning into it.

"Are the scars from..."

I nod. "Multiple places."

She ties the last one. "That does it."

I sit on the edge of the bed as she goes back to the chair. We sit for longer than I would expect since they were having a party when we showed up and obviously weren't busy.

"Do you think they're trying to get the doctor sober enough to stitch me?"

She leans back and crosses her long legs. "I think hospitals just make you wait forever for no reason. So you appreciate their time more?" She shrugs.

I lean on the bed and press the button for the television.

"Do you miss your family?" she asks. "Out there with Mags, you two seemed to understand each other so well."

I turn to look at Tessa. Now I'm convinced that my gut was right earlier and something is bothering her. She tries to come off as tough, but I think she might have a soft underbelly.

"I do. I'm usually so busy that I don't have time to think about it, but it's easier for us."

She leans forward and rests one elbow on her knee while placing her chin in her open palm. "I would think it would be harder for those serving."

I shake my head. "The people left behind are usually in the same place they remember us being for the holiday. Take my mom. She wakes up Christmas morning, and though my little brother and sister are there, she feels my absence. In every memory she has of Christmas, I'm there, in that house, so my absence is just as noticeable as if they had no tree on Christmas. Every tradition they do that holiday, I'm not there for it, and she feels it."

"That makes a lot of sense."

"Believe me, it sucks being away, but..." I shrug, unsure what else I could say.

"What do you miss the most?" she asks. "Not sugar cookies, I'm guessing?"

I chuckle. "I like sugar cookies, just not ones from a stranger. My mom would lecture me for days."

"Yeah, Gladys looks like the type to lace a sugar cookie." She grins and I stare at her for a beat.

"You can't trust her just because she's a grandma. The ones who get away with it are always the least suspicious."

Silence descends on us again. Our conversation isn't coming as naturally as I might hope, but we're not arguing so... progress, I guess.

"Eggnog," I blurt out.

"Eggnog is what you miss most?"

I nod. "I love eggnog, and my mom makes it the best. It's a family recipe. One day I'm going to get it."

Her eyes widen.

"Not the answer you'd think?"

She shakes her head. "I'm not sure what I thought, but good to know... eggnog. I saw some out there. Want a glass?"

"No thanks. I can wait until I get home. But could you see how much longer the wait is?"

She stands. "Want me to go *Terms of Endearment* for you?"

I don't tell her that I have no clue what she's talking about because she'll razz me for it, but she leaves the room. A short time later, she comes back with a doctor right behind her.

"Hi. I'm your doctor. Mags tells me you have a cut that might need stitches?"

I hold out my arm. "Yeah, here it is."

He washes his hands and puts on some gloves, eyeing Tessa the entire time.

"She didn't cut you, did she?" He laughs. Neither of us do, though in the short time we've known each other, I'm sure Tess has wanted to. "Just kidding. Your girlfriend looks too innocent."

"Oh, we're not…" Tessa is quick to tell him we're not a couple, which rankles though it shouldn't.

The doctor sits down on the roller stool and wheels over to me, all while looking at her. "Brother and sister?"

"Nope," she says. "Strangers traveling cross country together."

The doctor's eyes bulge out. I hate that she's telling him information he does not need to know. "Tell me how that happened."

Finally, he takes my arm to investigate the cut. He cleans it out and puts on antiseptic while listening to Tessa tell him the story.

"Mags!" he calls.

I get it's a small-town hospital, but a little professionalism would go a long way.

She walks in with a cup of eggnog in her hand. "Here you go." She leaves it on my tray on wheels.

"Definitely stitches, you were right. Want to set it up?" the doctor says.

"Sure thing." She turns to go to the cabinet to get everything together, then looks over her shoulder at me. "Want to be numbed?"

"Of course he does," Tessa answers for me at the same time I say, "Nah."

"Why not?" Tessa asks, leaning to the side to look around Mags, who's going back and forth from the supply cupboards.

"I've had plenty without anything."

"That one on your forehead probably needed some," Mags says.

"Come on, Mags, it's sexy." I waggle my eyebrows.

Tessa comes to the bedside. "I'm finding out all these new things about you. You love eggnog, and you can be a flirt."

"Hey, we have some cookies and stuff out here if you're hungry." The doctor looks at Tessa, waiting for an answer.

Great, he's going to whisk her away with the lure of sugar. I have a feeling it's like flowers and chocolates to her.

"Oh, cookies? Sure." Tessa turns to walk away but circles back. "Want me to bring you some?"

"Nah."

"Oh, that's right, sugar is the devil." She laughs and walks out of the room.

Mags stops setting up the tray and studies me for a long time. It's weird the connection I feel with her. Almost as if I knew her before I joined the armed forces. That sexy comment isn't anything I wouldn't say to someone unless I was close to them. It's hard to put my finger on.

"What's going on with you two?" She glances toward the door.

"I think that's a better question for the doctor."

Her head rears back. "Dr. John wouldn't steal your girl."

I laugh. "She's not my girl. I barely know her."

"Weird... doesn't seem like that. If I didn't know better, I'd say the two of you were close."

I shake my head. "Not at all. We were on the same plane to Portland, got to Minneapolis and the airport shut down, so now we're driving together because..." I don't finish my sentence because it sounds irresponsible to say my license has expired. And that's when I realize Mags reminds me of my mom.

"Sometimes things like this happen for a reason. Kismet."

I make a buzzer sound. "She's on her way to Portland looking for a second chance with her ex."

"Really?" Her eyebrows rise.

Just then, Tessa returns with a handful of cookies. Her cheeks are red which makes me think good ol' Dr. John might not be as innocent as Mags thinks he is. My jaw cocks to the side, and I inhale a deep breath—we'll be out of here in no time.

"Tell Mags about your psychic journey," I say to Tessa.

She puts the cookies next to the eggnog and picks one back up, biting into it immediately.

"Gossiping about my business, are we?" Tessa doesn't sound too perturbed.

"Mags thought we were a couple, and when I explained the situation, she thought it might be kismet for us, so I was explaining that a psychic says otherwise."

Tessa narrows her eyes, but there's amusement on her face that I kind of like. For a moment, I wonder what a life with someone who's my complete opposite would look like. Sure, I enjoy banter, but I think there'd be a lot of arguing, though neither of us seems to hold a grudge. She's clearly looking for love in her life—hell, she's traveling across the country for it—while I'm not so sure I believe in love. I saw a lot of guys think they found it until they left for basic or missions. Coming home to empty homes, rumors about their girlfriends or wives cheating with another soldier.

"So, a psychic, huh?" Mags asks her, dragging me from my thoughts.

Tessa sits back in her chair. "It was at a Christmas party. She told me she saw me alone in life unless I changed my ways, but said there was an opportunity to make it work with one man."

I sit up straighter, intrigued because this part she hasn't told me yet.

"Changed your ways?" Mags asks.

It's even more clear now how much like my mom she is. My mom would grill Tessa too.

"I tend to not give people a lot of time before I cut the cord. Always finding some fault with them, seeing signs that we shouldn't be together."

It's telling how perceptive Tessa is about herself to figure that out. I'd rather stab myself twenty times than do an internal audit about what's holding me back.

"Did she give you clues? There must be some reason you've picked this guy to travel so far for?"

Tessa sits for a moment and stares down at where her legs are crossed. "Well... she said he comes from a loving family and this particular guy was going home to visit his family for the holidays. Around Thanksgiving, my ex asked if I would join him for Christmas, but I declined for... reasons. And she said he helps a lot of people, and he works in IT, and he's always complaining about people and how it's the simplest fix. She said he had dark hair, which this guy does."

"So, she told you he has a close family, he helps people, and he has dark hair?" Mags sounds skeptical. I have to admit those aren't exactly concrete details you could add to a missing person's poster to identify someone.

"He's the last person I dated, and all those things are true of him. It has to be him."

Mags nods. "Well, I wish you luck. You clearly believe in fate, unlike this guy." She nods toward me. "Try to rub off on him for the rest of the trip."

Tessa laughs. "Believe me, he has opportunities everywhere

we go. You're the first woman I've seen him flirt with though." She winks.

Mags laughs.

"Can we stop talking about me like I'm not here? I'm not interested in a relationship right now."

Both women look at me but say nothing.

Dr. John comes in then, and again, he looks in Tessa's direction first. "Let's get these stitches in and get you guys back on the road, shall we?"

Mags is Dr. John's assistant, handing him tools as he needs them, and Tessa sits down, scrolling through her phone. I can't help but wonder if she's texting the guy in question, telling him she's on her way. Maybe I shouldn't have said no to the impromptu stops.

Then I remember I have enough on my damn plate. I don't need someone like Tessa to worry about—a woman who embarked on a trip with no money in her pocket, no backup plan, all because of a psychic reading.

Chapter Eleven

TESSA

Tre's all stitched up, and I'm ready to get back on the road, but Mags comes into the room, pushing another bed with blankets and pillows stacked high on top of it.

"Now, I'm a mother, and I don't want to hear no for an answer. You two are staying here and getting a good night's sleep." She maneuvers the bed beside the one Tre is on as though she moves furniture for a living when she's not nursing.

"We're already way behind for the day. Thank you for the kind offer, but we need to get going." Tre grabs his jacket to put on.

Mags continues to make the beds, putting multiple blankets over them both. They're only spaced about six inches apart because of the size of the room. Does she really expect me to sleep only six inches away from him?

"I told you I'm not taking no. I have your information and know who your emergency contact is. Don't make me call your mother, Abner."

I laugh at her referring to him by his legal name.

He stops mid motion, looks at her, then me. "HIPAA is a real thing, Mags."

"In any other hospital, I wouldn't be offering to let the two of you sleep here. Things here run a little differently." Mags puts her hands on her hips.

Tre puts his fingers through his hair and pulls at his neck.

"I already have a lot to worry about at night. Do you want me to add you two driving on dark, snow-covered highways to my list?"

"You're really giving me mom guilt?" Tre asks.

Kenzie complains about her mom a lot. Is that mom guilt? I don't think so. Whatever this is, I never had the pleasure of receiving it.

He's definitely going to cave, so I don't bother with my jacket but decide to sit on the bed because I really am tired.

"I'll do whatever it takes for you two to stay here. I work the night shift anyway. I just have to get you out by eight." Mags leaves the room.

Tre glances at me, question in his eyes.

"I am kind of tired. The airport wasn't comfortable, and I'm fairly sure there are no cockroaches here." I look at the floor to make sure.

"Fine, but we're leaving at five. I'll be back. I have to call my parents and fill them in."

He leaves the room, and I figure it's time I call the one person in the world who might be worried about me. I pull out my phone and pull up Kenzie's number. It rings twice, and I realize it's kind of late there.

"Hello," she says groggily. Maybe I should have waited until tomorrow. "Tess?"

"I'm sorry for calling a little late."

"Are you in Portland?" she asks. "You were supposed to call me, and I tried you a few times, but it went straight to voice mail."

"I haven't had the best reception, and no, I'm not in Portland." I cross my legs and sit on the bed, worried about receiving her wrath.

"Okay, you're being vague. What did you do? Cash in your ticket and go to the Caribbean? I don't blame you. I'm going to be honest, I'm not a huge fan of Carter."

"Kenz! I'm still on my way to see Carter."

"Damn, sorry, I always open my mouth too soon."

"It's okay as long as you don't lose it when I tell you where I am." I bite my nails. Not having a mom, Kenzie is the closest thing.

"Where are you? And stop biting your nails." She's fully awake now.

I hear Andrew grumbling.

"Just go to sleep, honey. I'll be right back. Hold on." I hear sheets rustle, then a door shut. "Okay, where are you?"

"I'm in South Dakota."

"Okay... why?"

"A woman went into labor on the plane, so it had to land in Minnesota, then there was a snowstorm that closed the airport, so I went down to rent a car, but they only had one left... and there was me and another guy who wanted it."

"Okkaayy..."

"His driver's license had expired and my credit card declined, so we kind of rented the car..."

"Together? You're traveling with a stranger across the country?" she shouts at me, and I pull the phone away from my ear. "You could be murdered on the side of the road right now."

"He's a soldier in the military, it's fine."

"So his hands are probably lethal weapons?"

Huh, I hadn't thought about that.

"How much money do you have?"

Shit, she always asks questions that get me in trouble. "He's agreed to pay for the entire trip."

Silence. Total silence.

"I'm taking a breath." I hear it through the receiver. "Okay, Tessa…" She takes another breath. "So, you've agreed to go cross country with a stranger who is in the military. Licensed to kill. And he's going to pay for you with no expectation of you paying him back."

"Well, obviously I'm going to." I fiddle with the blanket underneath me.

"But he's not expecting another kind of repayment?"

"Oh my god. No!" I screech. "He's not like that. We actually kind of hate one another. We get on each other's nerves."

"So, you don't like one another. That makes it better how?"

My shoulders slump and I stare at the other bed where he's going to sleep next to me all night. I haven't even told her how hot he is, how attractive I find him even though he annoys me half the time.

"Just… you can trust me. I can make good decisions." Even if recent history is no indicator of this.

More silence. Maybe I should remind her that her first date with Andrew, she showed up in an elf costume. Sometimes our decisions are questionable, but I would never put myself in harm's way.

Tre walks in and I bite the inside of my cheek since I'm still talking to her.

"And you're in South Dakota right now. What, in a hotel?"

"A hospital," I whisper, knowing what's coming.

"A hospital? Why?"

"There was an accident."

Tre's eyebrows raise and he smirks. It's the kind of smirk I can see him giving if he were hovering over me and about to slide inside. It is so damn hot.

"Meaning?" Kenzie asks.

"He stopped to go to the bathroom, I opened my door, and he tumbled down an embankment, cut himself, and we're here so he could get stitches."

I mouth *sorry* to Tre, but he waves me off.

"Let me talk to him," she says.

"No."

"Yes. He's there, I can tell. You're being quieter, so hand the phone over."

"No way."

"Tessa..."

If I don't hand him the phone now, she's going to probably call every hospital in South Dakota. Rarely does she let things go. I put her on mute. "My friend wants to talk to you. She thinks you could kill me with your bare hands because they're probably registered as weapons or something."

He chuckles and puts his hand out for the phone, surprising me. He unmutes it. "Kenzie, this is Tre." How the hell did he know her name? But then I realize it's on the screen. It bothers me that I can't hear what they're saying. "Army Ranger... long enough... no, I don't carry weapons with me... No, my hands aren't registered... I could if I wanted to... yes, she's only eaten sugar so far today..."

The conversation must be changing tone because he's laughing at whatever she's saying.

"Oh really?... She didn't tell me that... I get it... Of course... Sounds good..."

I'm thankful it sounds like the conversation is wrapping up.

"Red, huh?... I'll have to remember that... thanks for the tip... oh, I have no doubt... awesome... talk to you later... bye." He ends the call and hands me my phone.

"Do I even want to know what the red comment was about?"

"She said your favorite lingerie color is red." He sits in the chair, unties his boots, slips out of them, and tucks them under the chair.

I look at my boots that I tossed haphazardly below me. "She did not!"

"Nope. She said you love licorice and that you like to eat when you drive." He smiles as his fingers go to his belt.

I put up my hand, eyes wide. "What are you doing?"

"Come on, I know there's a sense of humor in there somewhere." He walks toward the bathroom and shuts the door.

"Did they give you happy drugs when they did the stitches?" I call.

Mags comes in.

"Did you give him some happy drugs?"

She smiles. "No." She puts a few supplies into the cabinet in the room. "That psychic didn't say anything about a sense of humor, huh?"

"I know you think I'm delusional."

Mags puts up her hand. "I think it's romantic. I think few people take the chance you're taking to find love. Own it, Tessa. It's admirable to be so forthcoming with what you want in life."

My cheeks heat a bit. "Thanks."

Tre comes out of the bathroom wearing just pajama pants. Mags stops and stares at him and for good reason. He could be in a fitness magazine.

"Good night," she says.

"Good night," he returns.

Once we're in bed, I look at the frame of his body. He's on his back with one arm tucked under his head.

"Why did you give in so easily?" I whisper.

"Because she reminds me of my mom. I've put her

through hell all these years I've been gone. So if having me here makes her remember what it's like to care for her boy, then I'll do it."

"Huh. You're really sweet under that tough exterior."

For a moment, he doesn't say anything. "I'm not that tough. Believe me."

And then neither of us speaks again and eventually sleep comes because it's been one long day.

I stretch my arms and legs like in a movie. I don't remember the last time I slept that well. I didn't wake up to go to the bathroom or from some weird dream or anything. I look to my left to see if Tre is already awake. Except Tre isn't there and his bed is made.

Shut up. He left me.

I bolt upright in bed and throw off the covers, realizing my shirt became skewed at some point, so I straighten that, grab my shoes, and search for my purse and belongings.

Here I thought we were starting to trust each other. I didn't think he'd leave me stranded in South Dakota. What kind of soldier does that?

I open the door and look out into the hallway. The hospital must have a busy morning. There are more doctors and more nursing staff around than last night. I spot some Santas on stretchers outside rooms, Mrs. Clauses by their sides telling them to be quiet.

Before I can look down the hallway in the other direction, two hands push me back into the room.

"What the hell?" I say.

The door shuts, and it's Tre. I don't want to examine why I feel an immense amount of relief.

"We don't want to get Mags in trouble, so we need to get

out of here quietly." He tosses whatever was in his hand on the table and sits down, putting on his boots.

"What's going on out there?" I whisper, shoving on my coat.

"From what I overheard, there was some Santa and Mrs. Claus contest at a bar in the neighboring town last night, and things got out of hand and turned into a Santa brawl." He shrugs on his jacket. "Alcohol always brings out the worst in people."

"I thought you left," I admit for reasons I'm not sure.

He stops and looks at me, hurt flashing in his eyes. "Mags brought us black coffee, but I went to get some cream and sugar for you."

I stand with my jaw open and, if I'm honest, my heart open too. He remembered how I take my coffee.

"The only thing I didn't know is whether you really take two sugars or if you just added that second one yesterday to stick it to me over the whole sugar comment." He raises one eyebrow, and I laugh quietly.

"You can read people way too well, do you know that?"

He shrugs. "Kind of comes with the job. I have to make some quick decisions."

I'm curious to know, but I don't ask him what his first thought of me was. I have to remind myself that just because he remembers how I take my coffee doesn't mean anything. Any good barista can remember that too.

Chapter Twelve

TRE

After a quick goodbye to Mags, we leave the hospital. I drive for a while until we pull off the highway to get gas, food, and to stretch our legs.

"What do you think? Should we try to go all the way?" I ask while I gather all the trash in the car to throw out in the gas station garbage.

She's just returning from the bathroom. "I can take the shift, but the GPS said it's almost another sixteen hours."

"Hard to believe we left yesterday, and we've only gotten eleven hours into the drive, huh?" I toss the trash and finish refueling.

"Well, we did sleep somewhere last night." She looks at the diner beside the gas station. "I'm going to be honest with you, I cannot eat diner food again."

Unfortunately, most of the exits are a local diner or fast food with not much in between.

"How do you know? They might be famous for their apple pie or something?"

She narrows her eyes, but there's a playfulness that isn't always there. "I really want a big juicy burger."

A car pulls up to the pump next to ours and a family files out. "Quick bathroom break, you guys. I told you to go before we left so you didn't have to before we got to the Eggnog Festival."

Tessa's head turns as fast as a cat who spotted a mouse.

Fuck, I've done so well keeping her on task even after we passed the Minuteman Missile National Historic Site, where she pleaded that admission was free, then the Dinosaur Park and the Reptile Gardens. And then she went on and on and told me that I'm not a true American when I refused to go off course to see Mount Rushmore. Truthfully, I almost caved on that one because it is something I want to see, but the weather is only getting colder, and I don't want us to get stranded anywhere. Not much has gone our way.

"Did you say Eggnog Festival?" Tessa steps over the edge of our pump and asks the mom.

Damn it, she's going to whine about this one too. Surely the words fate and kismet are going to come again.

"Yeah, it's an annual festival, only today and tomorrow, but tonight is when everyone brings their eggnog to try to win the ribbon." The woman opens up the back of her conversion van, and I briefly wonder if they even make those anymore. She pulls out two jugs, holding them out as if she's already won. "These are ours."

"Interesting. So, you just go taste eggnog?"

"Oh no, there's a whole festival. Great big barrels filled with huge fires to stay warm, live music, face painting, crafts for the kids. There's a Santa and his elves, a lot of tasting booths and the competition. A whole Christmas market." She smiles widely as though she can't wait to get there.

"Don't forget the chugging competition," her husband chimes in, filling his tank with about four times what we bought. "Always at the end of today. It all used to be held on Christmas Eve since that's National Eggnog Day, but too many people would miss celebrating the holidays with their families, so they moved it to the weekend before."

"You two should go. It's once-in-a-lifetime fun," the wife says.

Their kids barrel out of the gas station, running into the van screaming eggnog over and over.

Tessa shoots me a look. One that says we need to go. This is a sign that we ran into these people.

Damn it all to hell. I should've insisted she stay in the car to stay warm when she was done using the bathroom.

"Tell you what? Here are two tickets. Since we run a booth and enter the contest, we get in for free, but we're given two tickets to give to whoever. Usually we just pick two people outside before they buy tickets, but you seem really excited." The dad holds them out.

Tessa snatches them out of his hand as if they're hundred-dollar bills. "Thank you."

"I'm not sure if we're going," I say.

All three of them turn toward me as though I'm ruining the fun they have planned.

"We have a long drive back to Portland."

Tessa leans forward and whispers something I can't hear. The man and woman smile, watching Tessa pocket the tickets. I grab the receipt for the gas, and I'm about to walk over to the driver's side when Tessa runs over and opens the door.

"My turn to drive, remember?" she shouts, securing herself in the seat with her seat belt on.

I open the passenger door and peer in. "I'm not an idiot. We are not going to the Eggnog Festival, Tessa. It'll cost us another night, and what if another storm comes through? We still have a long drive to get home."

"You said so yourself. You miss eggnog the most. Come on, this is fate."

I stand and stare at the sky. There's that fucking word

again. *Fate.* "Tessa, it's not fate. It's not kismet. It's that we stopped right down the street from the festival. You wouldn't even have known about it if that couple hadn't stopped next to us."

"Exactly my point. Come on. You deserve this. I got us free tickets. It'll be so much fun. We'll go, you can drink eggnog, I'll stay sober, and after an hour, we'll get back on the road. I napped so I can drive through the night no problem."

I blow out a breath and stare at her, but she takes her finger and crosses her heart, then juts out her bottom lip in a way that makes me want to suck on it.

"Promise. An hour."

With a sigh, I climb into the car. I'm not usually one who backs down, but I have missed good eggnog, and it's not like I'll ever come back here again. "Fine. An hour only. And this is the last detour."

"Last detour." She salutes me, and I shake my head at her then stare ahead.

"Let's go."

"Yay!" She does a little dance in her seat and starts the car.

We head out of the gas station and follow the signs to the Eggnog Festival.

* * *

"Are you sure this is a parking spot?" I ask Tessa because we aren't parked in the big fenced-off area like almost everyone else. Turns out the Eggnog Festival is held just off their small town square in a big field that I imagine is used for planting some vegetation during the warmer months.

"Yes. Another sign of fate. It's so easy to get in and get out."

I nod and step out of the car, putting on my jacket and sliding my hat over my head. Tessa puts on a hat with a pom-

pom on top. Although her hair hasn't been nicely styled the way it was the first time I saw her at the airport, her natural beauty shines bright.

We walk across the street and Tessa hands our tickets to the teenager who's more concerned about talking with her friends than who's coming in.

Surprisingly in these parts, the cold doesn't keep people inside. Everyone from their town must be in attendance there are so many people here. A band's playing next to a few booths serving alcohol other than eggnog.

"Come on, let's get you some." Her gloved hand grabs mine, and she pulls me toward the tasting. She stops in front of the first booth, which happens to have a middle-aged woman running it. "This is Tre, he's a soldier and hasn't drunk eggnog in…" She stares at me.

"A long time."

"Right." She covers her mouth, trying to hide a smile, I think. "He has to keep a lot of stuff confidential."

I roll my eyes.

"We're on our way to Oregon but ran into a couple at the gas station who told us about this event. They're here somewhere, entering the contest."

"Get on with it, Tessa," I murmur.

"Yes, anyway, can he have a taste?"

The middle-aged woman laughs. "You may." She hands me a small Dixie cup filled to the brim with the pale yellow liquid.

I sip it and hand it to Tessa, who refuses. "I'm driving."

"Right."

That's the smart thing to do, but then I look at the long line of booths. There's no way I'm going to taste all these by myself, and what, describe them to her? Why should I be the only one to have fun? It's obvious Tessa likes to partake in these kinds of things.

"How was the cinnamon?" she asks, looking at me expectantly.

I finish the eggnog. "Have some. We'll figure out a place to stay. I don't want to experience this all by myself."

"You aren't by yourself. Look at all these people." She circles around with her arms open. "You all love eggnog."

"You know what I mean." I lower my voice so only she can hear me.

Our eyes meet and hold.

"But it will delay us." Her voice is soft and unsure.

"I don't care. Share tonight with me. Do you like eggnog?"

She smiles brightly, and I swear I feel my heart expand in my chest. "Who doesn't?" She accepts a cup from the woman and downs it like a shot.

We head to the next booth and move down the line until we're eggnogged out and decide to head toward the food.

"Excuse me?" Someone approaches us as we each get a pretzel with cheese.

We turn to find a woman dressed in Christmas lights. Literally just a skintight spandex thing with lights wrapped around her and a star as a hat.

"Are you in the military?" she asks me.

"Yes, he is," Tessa answers for me, chewing a large piece of the pretzel.

"We had a competitor who got sick, and we need another volunteer for the eggnog chugging contest. A few of the booth renters told us you serve and how much you love eggnog, but it's been so long since you've had it. We'd be honored if you'd participate."

"Oh well..."

"What an honor. He'll do it," Tessa says on my behalf.

"I will?" I look at her.

"Yep. Where does he need to be?"

I can't very well say no to this nice woman, and Tessa looks so excited about my involvement.

"Great! It starts in about fifteen minutes. Over there under the green tent." She points in the direction, and I nod.

"I'll be there."

She walks away, and I groan.

"We could have made an excuse. I can't chug anything," I say under my breath.

"Why? I drank too, so we're here for the night. Might as well enjoy it."

"Which brings up the question of where we're going to stay?" Knowing her, she won't worry about it until the night is over.

"I'll find us a place. You open up that gullet and let it flow down like a beer funnel." She puts her arm through mine and walks us toward the green tent.

I'm not sure how much alcohol was in the eggnog, but she's clearly kind of tipsy. She's even more live in the moment than usual, which I wouldn't have thought was possible.

Once we get to the tent, she raises on her tiptoes and whispers in my ear, "I'll be in the audience, cheering you on."

"What if I throw up?" I ask, but she's already disappeared into the crowd.

The Christmas tree lady introduces me to her husband, who I'm told is the winner for the last five years. He's got me by a hundred pounds and six inches. He's a monster of a man. The other competitor is a little woman, probably in her forties with a kid wrapped around her waist. My competitive instincts roar to life when I spot Tessa in the crowd.

We sit at a table and are introduced to the crowd by the Christmas tree lady.

"First up, we have Little Becky, mother of four with the jaws of a shark."

The crowd cheers for her, some hoots and hollers ringing out.

"Second up, we have a newbie to the festival this year. Rumor is he's an Army Ranger and has been without eggnog or at least a decent eggnog for a while. Let's cross our fingers he's not one-and-done tonight."

People laugh, but Tessa stands on a chair and whoops with her fist in the air, screaming for me. I shake my head at her and laugh.

"That's his sweet girlfriend."

Tessa freezes for a second and our eyes meet, but neither of us corrects her.

"Third, my darling husband. Five-year champ and soon to be six, Round Rowdy."

He waves and the crowd goes crazy. He's clearly the fan favorite.

Eggnog pitchers are set in front of each of us.

"All right, whoever drinks the most pitchers in the time frame is the winner. Ready, everyone?"

We all nod.

"Go."

I swear Rowdy downs two before I finish one. Even Little Becky is going faster than me.

"Go, Tre!" Tessa cheers.

I try to chug and chug, but Jesus, this is a lot of dairy.

I'm on my third pitcher when Rowdy asks for another with four empties in front of him. There's no way I'm going to beat him, so I turn to Little Becky. She's on her third as well, but still ahead of me, but only by a little. The kid on her hip stares at me for a moment then raises his middle finger at me.

What the hell?

Another pitcher goes down, and my stomach churns,

rumbling and sour. I have to swallow back the liquid coming up my throat.

When I look up, Tessa is right in front of me. "Come on, Tre, you got this. You're a Ranger. Show them what that means."

I shake my head because I'm seriously going to die if I ingest any more of this stuff.

Rowdy slows finally, and Little Becky is only sipping now.

"You got this," Tessa says again.

Everything inside me tells me to stop, but I close my eyes and remember basic, remember Ranger school, how I never thought I'd get through that. My throat muscles burning, my heart pounding, I ask for another pitcher, which will put me at the same number as Rowdy.

Little Becky shakes her head, hands off her kid to her husband, and throws up in the bucket we're each given.

Rowdy and I are both on our fifth, and Christmas tree lady tries to keep him going, but he turns and throws up all over her.

"You won!" Tessa's eyes widen. "He wins, right?"

"He has to keep it down for five minutes," Christmas tree lady says, cringing at what's covering her.

I shake my head to Tessa. There's no way I can do that.

"You can." She nods and points at a sign. The winner of the chugging contest wins a night's stay at the Jingle Balls B&B tonight.

My head rocks back and I keep my mouth shut. The clock ticks down, and I watch it the entire time. Three minutes left. I put my hand on my stomach because it hurts so much. I cough, and everyone holds their breath, thinking this is it.

"You got this. You're the toughest guy I know. This is all you, Tre. All you," Tessa says, and I close my eyes. I can't disappoint her.

A millisecond after the five minutes has passed, the bell

rings, and I bury my head in the bucket, throwing up for at least five minutes.

But I won the gift certificate, and the look on Tessa's face makes it all worth it. I can't remember the last time someone looked at me like that. Maybe never. But definitely too fucking long.

Chapter Thirteen

TESSA

Lucky for us, Jingle Balls B&B is just on the other side of the town square, so we can leave the car where it is and walk over. I grab our bags from the back, including the garbage bag with the uniform he wore on the airplane. I'm hoping the kind owners at Jingle Balls will let me wash them for him. Especially since he did a chugging competition to win us this room.

Tre is still sitting on the stairs of the front porch of the B&B when I return, leaning his head on the iron banister and looking really green.

"How are you feeling?" I ask.

He stands as I approach, following me inside.

"Don't ask," he grumbles. "This better be worth it."

I walk over to the desk where an older woman with a head of gray hair is looking at us with anticipation. "I was expecting you," she says with a huge smile.

"Were you there?"

She shakes her head. "No, but I heard about it."

"That was fast. Small towns, huh?" I say. "We're lucky you were giving the room for the night."

She winks and grabs a pencil to write something in a little book. "Sometimes it can feel like magic when things work out perfectly."

Oh, if I had gotten to have a grandma in my life, I would've wanted this one. She is so adorable.

"I have some cookies in the kitchen. I was just frosting them. I could make some coffee or tea or hot cocoa." She looks past me to Tre, sitting in one of the red chairs next to the perfectly decorated Christmas tree as if every ornament was placed for a reason. The white lights glisten on the tinsel hanging off the tree. "Or eggnog," she whispers, but not quietly enough because Tre groans.

"I think he's going to shower and go straight to bed," I say.

"Save your appetite then because there will be a big breakfast tomorrow morning."

"We have to leave at sunrise, but thank you for having us tonight. It's a beautiful home with so much holiday spirit."

Tre comes up behind me, whispering, "Let's go."

"Yes, this town loves Christmas. Most of our guests come between Thanksgiving and Christmas, then we have regulars that do Christmas in July. Kind of odd when you see a Santa Claus setting off fireworks." She laughs and slides the key across the desk. "I put you guys in the Nutcracker room. It's one of my favorites."

"Sounds painful," Tre mumbles.

"Great. Thanks again. I honestly can't convey how much of a lifesaver this is."

She smiles, and her hand, covered with age spots and wrinkles, squeezes mine. "We're very happy to have you."

"Good night..." I pause, not knowing what to call her.

"Mrs. Kringle, of course."

Tre groans behind me.

"Good night, Mrs. Kringle."

"Good night, may visions of sugar plums dance in your heads." She smiles.

I giggle, and Tre lightly nudges me toward the stairs.

"Oh, I almost forgot. Is there a washer and dryer I could use?" I turn to ask.

"How about you give them to me to start while you two get settled?"

This woman is a godsend. "Thank you." I hand over the bag of clothes. "I'll be right back after he changes out of these."

"Perfect. It's just off the kitchen to the right," she says and walks that way.

"Um…" Tre meets my gaze. "Those are my fatigues."

"She's a grandma. I'm sure she knows how to wash them better than me."

"That's exactly why I was going to do them myself."

I climb the stairs without looking back at him. "Isn't it nice when you can rely on others?"

"Until the fatigues come back doll size."

I shake my head at the top of the stairs and search for which room is the Nutcracker room.

"We couldn't be in the candy cane room or winter wonderland?" he says.

"Oh relax." I insert the key and open the door, pausing in the doorway.

"What? Why did you stop?" He looks in the room over my head. "Told you."

The room is filled with nutcrackers, *so* many nutcrackers, all staring at us from different angles.

"And to think you couldn't sleep because of a cockroach. Now we have a hundred sets of eyes on us." He slides past me, and I swallow hard.

"It's a room, and it's free, and we're going to make the most of it."

"And the queen bed." He stands at the foot of it and gestures to it. "We gonna make the most of that too?" He waggles his brows in a way that lets me know he's kidding.

A flash of disappointment bolts through me. Which is ridiculous because I'm on my way to make amends with another man.

"Funny." I give him a saccharine smile. "We'll figure it out. Now you go shower."

He grabs his bag and heads down the hall to the shower while I sit on the edge of the bed, wondering if I could find something wrong with the room so the woman downstairs would change it for us. I don't want to be ungrateful, but these wooden figures staring at me is creepy as all hell.

I grab some clothes for my shower once Tre is done. I find some blankets in the closet, so I roll them and place them in the center of the bed, so there will be no touching. Because it's really starting to hit me that I'm going to be sharing a bed with a gorgeous, muscled single man tonight.

Once I'm satisfied that the little barrier will work, I realize that Tre has been in the shower a long time. I knock on the bathroom door so I can grab his clothes to add them to the wash Mrs. Kringle is starting. But I realize that the water's not on, and he opens it up a little, steam filtering out. His dark hair is damp and falling on his forehead while droplets of water slide down his nose to the floor.

"Sorry, I just thought I'd grab your clothes and fatigues to wash them."

"Oh yeah, thanks."

He turns around, and all he's wearing is a white towel wrapped around his waist. I admire his ass as he bends over and picks up the clothes stacked in a pile in the corner of the room. The dark hair that sprinkles his chest makes me wonder what it would feel like to run my fingers through it as I lie next to him in bed. Or what it might feel like against my breasts as he slid inside me.

"Here." He hands them to me.

His voice brings me out of my daydream, and I blink. "Thanks," I mumble, certain I look like a drooling crazy woman staring at his chest.

"Are you okay?" His forehead wrinkles.

My cheeks heat. "I'm good. Just... I'll be back." I turn my back to him and head down the stairs, where I find Mrs. Kringle decorating cookies.

"Hi, dear, put those next to the washer. I'll handle it all."

"That's not necessary."

"Yes, it is. I miss having kids to take care of, so humor me. Plus, as the wife of a retired police officer, it's been a long time since I've had to iron a uniform. Now, take this plate of cookies up to your room. Nothing helps a good night's sleep like sugar."

I stare at her decorated sugar cookies. There isn't one mistake, between the Santa's red cheeks to the reindeer's dark eyes. "They're too beautiful to eat."

She chuckles. "Nothing is too beautiful to eat."

I have a bunch of questions I want to ask her. Like does she prefer the thinner cookie versus a thicker? What does she think makes the perfect sugar cookie? But she'll probably ask me why and I don't want to get into why I know so much about baking.

"Thanks a lot... for everything." I head back upstairs and open the door of our room.

Tre is standing there in only his boxer briefs. I shut the door immediately and hear him howling with laughter behind the thick wood.

"You can open the door now, Rapunzel."

I open the door but look at the other side of the room from him. "Why Rapunzel?"

"Because she was innocent. Stuck up in that tower and didn't experience much. You looked so shocked and scandalized when you saw me in my briefs. But you can look now, I'm in my sweats."

I glance at him. "Still without a shirt."

"If you think I'm wearing a shirt to bed, you're crazy. You're lucky I'm wearing sweats. It's, like, a hundred degrees in here." He lies on the bed, and I pretend to be busy grabbing my clothes.

"I brought up some cookies. I'm going to take a shower."

I hurry out of the room and lock myself in the bathroom. I'm traveling across the country for another man. I have to remember that. Though it's not like Tre would want me anyway. I'm pretty sure he finds me annoying.

I shower, dry off, and put on the shorts and T-shirt set, thankful I didn't just bring my shorts and tank silk sets. I'm hoping he's asleep and I can sneak my way into the room and slide into bed without him noticing, so I slowly turn the doorknob and inch it open.

The lights are still on and he's on his phone, so I push the door open the rest of the way. "Not tired?"

He yawns. "Getting there. Just texting my family to say we're staying the night somewhere again."

He shuts off his phone while I stuff my dirty clothes into my bag and pull back the covers to get into bed.

"I like the barrier you put between us." He chuckles.

"Thanks."

Both of us click the lights off by our heads, then I turn on my side to face away from him, but I swear I can feel the plethora of nutcrackers staring at me in the dark.

"Good thing we're not a couple," I say.

"Why's that?"

"Because I can't imagine having sex with all these wooden statues staring at us."

He laughs, and the sound echoes in the dark, feeling like a warm caress.

"Did you have a cookie?" I ask.

"No."

"Why not?"

He's quiet for a beat. "It's embarrassing."

I roll over to face him, but it's dark, so I only see a shadow of him. "Tell me."

"I'm not giving up any information without you doing the same."

I blow out a breath. "Fine, but you answer first."

"I promised my mom I wouldn't eat a sugar cookie until I get home. It's just this big thing at our house ever since I was little. My mom plans an entire night of cutting them out, baking them, and decorating them."

"That's so sweet."

"It means a lot to her. It's weird, but ever since I went into the military, I feel like I broke her. She's always so worried. Reading the newspapers, watching the news, calling me and telling me what could happen. I could be shipped here or there. When I decided on Army Ranger, my dad thought it was great, but I saw it in my mom's face—the fear. So if not eating a sugar cookie even though I fucking love them is important to her, then I'll wait until we're together again."

Tears well up in my eyes, but I suck them back. I don't know what it's like to have someone like that in your life. To have someone care about you that much. "That wasn't the answer I was prepared for."

"Didn't think so. Now it's your turn in the hot seat."

"What do you want to know?"

He's quiet for a second, and I worry that he might have fallen asleep. "Name the shittiest thing to happen to you this year, other than some schmuck stealing your seat in first class?"

115

I smile since he probably can't even see me. "I feel like you set me up." I've been vocal about my life sucking recently, but not in specifics.

"You seemed really upset about the seat, but you've been going with the flow since we got snowed in at the airport. Makes me think there's a lot more to the story."

Do I tell him or keep it to myself? We're only traveling a little bit longer together. Then we'll go our separate ways. But he's easy to talk to, and after the story he just told me about his mom, I know he cares about others. So I opt for honesty.

"I had to close my bakery in New York. It was my dream for so long, but it's hard to make it there. Rent is so high, there's so much competition..."

"I'm sorry." His voice is soft and full of sympathy.

"Thanks."

We're quiet for a while, then he breaks the silence.

"I feel it sometimes when we're alone and neither of us are talking," he says quietly.

"You feel what?" I'm almost afraid to ask.

"Your sadness."

A tear slips from my eye, but I quickly turn back around and wipe it away. "We should go to bed."

Neither of us says anything for a long time.

"Good night," he whispers eventually.

But I pretend as if I've already fallen asleep.

Chapter Fourteen

TRE

I wake up as a stream of light peeks through the curtain.

It takes me a moment to register the warmth pressed to the front of my body—it isn't something I'm used to when I wake up. I'm a "kick the covers off in the middle of the night" sleeper. But the soft skin under my hand, the ass wiggling in my crotch, this is all new.

Oh shit.

I peek through one eye, and sure enough, I'm spooning Tessa. I'm not sure what my hand was doing, but she's moaning and squirming. Retracting my hand is torture, but she's going to freak out if she wakes up and sees the position we're in. Especially since my dick didn't get the memo that this is a platonic sleeping situation. When I roll onto my back, she rolls to her stomach, sliding her arms under her pillow and bending one knee up.

Once I'm not attached to her like a monkey, I sit up and look at her. The underside of her right ass cheek sticks out of her pajama bottoms, and her shirt has lifted enough that I know her stomach is exposed on the mattress.

She's so damn hot, I have no idea how I've been able to

keep my attraction hidden. Her following some guy across the country isn't really something that would have stopped me before. I'd shoot my shot and see what happened. But my military training runs deep, and I can deny myself if it's what's best. It's like we're on a mission and we have to depend on the ones alongside us. We're a team, and if we cross that line, we'd compromise the mission.

Once I'm out of bed, I position the blanket wall that's half crushed and pooled at our feet back into place. No reason she has to know how close we were last night.

It's easy to see that she's had a rough go of it lately, what with knowing her better now and looking back on how she acted when she found me in her first-class seat. Didn't help that I acted like a complete dick. But when she told me about her bakery, I heard the grief in her voice, but mostly I heard hopelessness. I'd like to get deeper into it sometime before this road trip is done, especially since I feel like maybe she's chasing this guy, not because she loves him but for a completely different reason.

I leave her sprawled out on the bed rather than waking her so we can get on the road right away. Then I grab my bag, change in the bathroom, and head downstairs.

Mrs. Kringle is in the kitchen, cooking. I knock on the doorframe to avoid startling her, but she still steps back from the stove with her hand over her heart, gasping.

"Oh goodness, you scared me. Tre, right?"

I nod.

She catches me reading her apron that says, "Let's Get Baked." "It was a gift from my grandson. He didn't quite understand the meaning, just thought of his grandma and baking."

"Makes sense. How old is he?" I take an egg from the carton resting on the counter and crack it into a bowl.

She points at the carton of eggs. "A dozen scrambled. And he's five. We've been blessed with many grandchildren."

I finish cracking the eggs and use the fork she puts out for me to whisk them. "Do they live around here?"

"One does. This town doesn't offer much for people with big dreams." She looks around her kitchen decorated with smartass signs like, "How do you like your eggs? In a cake." It's definitely her space and no one else's. "It's small, and Christmas isn't for everyone. We try to get out and visit our other kids, but we run a B&B." She shrugs.

I continue to scramble and walk the bowl over to a hot pan. "Who's all this for? You feeding a whole platoon?"

She laughs. "What you guys don't finish, I'll take over to the firehouse. They can always use a good meal."

I cook the eggs on the burner, slowly like my dad taught me on Sunday mornings when he cooked our family breakfast so our mom could sleep in.

They're about halfway done when I hear footsteps barrel down the stairs.

"I think she's up." Mrs. Kringle laughs.

We both turn toward the doorway, and sure enough, Tessa skids to a stop, heaving for a breath. "You." She points at me with an accusatory finger.

"What?" My eyebrows raise.

"You've got to stop leaving me..." She pants and inhales a deep breath. "In the morning. I keep thinking you've left me."

"I'm just helping to cook you breakfast." I motion to the pan filled with eggs on the stove.

"Sweetie, go take a shower, then come on down to eat. It's almost ready." Mrs. Kringle points toward the staircase.

Tessa lets out another long breath. "Okay, yeah."

Then she stares at me as if she needs reassurance I'm not going to leave her. I nod, and she turns around.

After we hear her walk back up the stairs, Mrs. Kringle

comes over to the stove with the pancake batter. She warms the skillet and puts pats of butter on the hot surface.

"She's been left before, I take it?" she asks me in a tone of voice as if she asked me what the weather was supposed to be like today.

"Um... I don't know everything, but the way she freaks out, I'd say yes."

"That's a hard one to get over. You two aren't a couple, are you?"

I shake my head. I'm sure she assumed, and maybe we could have asked her if there was another room available because we aren't a couple, but it didn't sit right with me to ask for a second room when we weren't even paying for the first.

"Yeah, I didn't think so."

"Why?" I ask, the crease between my eyebrows deepening.

"Forgive me for saying so, but sweetie, if you were my boyfriend, looking the way you do and all that, we wouldn't be leaving the bed until lunch."

I clear my throat and feel my cheeks heat.

"And because if you were her boyfriend, I don't think she'd be so fearful of being left. You remind me of my eldest. I'm not sure if it's because he had younger siblings, but he just knew how to nurture, you know. I think you do too, and if she were yours, she'd know there's no chance you'd cast her aside. All that doubt inside her wouldn't be there if you were hers." She shrugs. "Just a feeling. But what do I know, I'm just an old lady." She turns her head to look at me and winks.

"She's actually on her way to meet a guy, an ex of hers. Wants to surprise him." Even I can hear the mild irritation in my voice.

Her eyes widen, and she flips the first round of pancakes. "Well, lucky him then, I guess, huh?"

She doesn't look at me for a reaction. I'm not even sure

why she's saying it, but I feel like a million little needles are poking my skin all at once when I envision Tessa running toward him, all excited to see him again. I shake my head because I don't need the baggage of all her problems. I have enough of my own.

* * *

After breakfast, Tessa waves to Mrs. Kringle, thanking her again for use of the room and for breakfast.

"Thank you so much," I say, surprised when Mrs. Kringle steps into me with her arms open. I hug her, but not as tightly as she hugs me.

"It's never too late," she whispers.

I pull back from her, and both her gray eyebrows are raised. "Sorry?"

"To change the future. It's not etched in stone like the past."

I nod even if I'm not sure what she's talking about. "Thanks again."

We walk out of the Jingle Balls B&B and the cold hits us like a punch in the face. Tessa runs across the street toward the car, clearly wanting to get out of this cold as fast as possible. I carry my bag that's filled with my newly ironed fatigues and fresh laundry, grateful to Tessa and Mrs. Kringle for their help.

"Tre!" Tessa screams from around the corner.

I smile to myself, wondering what on earth is wrong now. Is there a reindeer on top of our car? I turn the corner and stop in my tracks, staring at where Tessa's twirling around where the car *used* to be parked, mouth gaping open.

"Where's the car?" I ask.

She stops and stares at me, her eyes boring into mine.

"Yeah, stupid question."

I look around and spot the police station on the other corner of the square.

"Let's head to the police station. We might have to report it stolen." I start walking, and she groans, following me.

"Why would someone steal that car? I mean, it's a death-trap on wheels." Her voice is raising.

This has really set her off even though she's the one who's ready to take detours. Maybe she's getting eager to reach our destination so she can meet up with her ex.

My hands fist at the thought. "Just relax. I can handle this." I open the door to the police station for her, but she doesn't walk through. Instead, she again glares at me.

"You can handle it? Because little ol' me can't? Is that because I have a vagina?"

I inhale a deep breath and let my eyes drift shut for a moment. "I only meant because you seem like you're about to come undone, and we don't need to piss them off."

"Huh, I see. Well, Mister Calm, Cool, and Collected, you go right ahead." She waves with an arm outstretched, and I walk into the police station first.

"Look who it is," Rowdy says. "Last night's winner."

"Oh shit," Tessa says under her breath when she registers that he's wearing a police uniform.

"Hey, Rowdy, right?" I approach him and hold out my hand, which he doesn't shake. "We were parked along the square in the northeast corner, but our vehicle is gone. We're not sure if it was stolen or what."

"You come here for one night and steal my championship, and now you're accusing one of our residents of being thieves?" He crosses his big arms, and another guy comes to stand alongside him.

"We don't steal things, especially matchbox cars," the other officer chimes in.

Off to a great start, I see. Awesome.

"Okay then, do you have any idea where it might have gone?" I'm wondering if these two took it somewhere as payback for me winning the chugging contest. Towed it behind the building as some joke on us.

"I'm not sure where you're from, but around here, no one but Judge Sullivan parks in his spot."

"Judge Sullivan," Tessa says. "It didn't say anything like that. How were we to know?"

"She's right. When we parked, there wasn't a sign anywhere."

"So now we're liars *and* thieves?" Rowdy asks.

I place my stuff on the wooden bench and walk up to him. "It was an honest mistake. We're not from here."

"Nope, you're not," Rowdy says.

"I'm assuming from what you're saying, is that our car got towed?"

"Smart one you are," the tall thin guy says.

"How much do we need to pay to get it out?" I ask, pulling out my wallet.

"Don't pay them, this is ridiculous. There was no sign." Tessa comes up next to me.

"Try looking for a sign in the snow, lady." The tall one gets his face right into Tessa's. "Because it's there now."

"No, it's not." She stomps out of the police station, and I close my eyes and take a deep breath.

"I'm going to show it to her." Rowdy's coworker follows her, and I walk out after them, watching from the stairs of the police station.

Their voices echo in the vacant square as they argue about whether or not there is a sign, when I hear Tessa say, "Oh, I see. But it wasn't there last night!"

"Woman, you think we could get a pole in this frozen ground overnight?"

They argue the whole way back.

123

"You better get your lady in line," Rowdy says when he comes out to stand beside me.

"My lady?" I arch an eyebrow.

"Henry doesn't take any shit, and she's piling it on pretty thick right now."

Once they're at the bottom of the stairs, I give Tessa a look to say calm down, but she breezes right by me, and pokes the tall officer in the back.

"Excuse me."

He turns around and towers over her.

She puts up her hands. "Fine. There was a sign, and I clearly missed it. The snow was covering it, but isn't there a ticket to be paid, or did you tow us?"

The tall guy crosses his arms and smirks at Rowdy. "Yeah, and it's gonna cost you all in all about five hundred between the ticket and fee for the tow and storage."

Tessa's mouth drops open. "That's ridiculous. You knew where we were. You could've come and asked us to move it. You're doing all this because he beat your friend last night." She pokes him in the chest. "Grow the hell up."

Oh shit.

The tall one looks at Rowdy, and he nods.

"Turn around, miss." The other officer has a smirk as though he's enjoying this.

"I'm not turning around," Tessa says. "You can't play with people just because this is some small town. You can't make up your own rules as you go to suit you."

He takes her elbow and turns her around.

"Hey," I say, going over to stop him. "You don't have to arrest her. I'll pay the fee, and we'll get out of your town. I promise we'll never return."

Meanwhile, Tessa is wiggling to get free as he cuffs her, going on and on about her rights.

How did this get so out of hand so quickly?

"I can't believe you're arresting me. This is complete bull-shit," Tessa says as he walks her down the hall.

I approach Rowdy, who's chuckling to himself. "How much to get her out and get the car back?"

He full-out laughs at me, and my jaw clenches, fists tightening at my sides. "Might as well head over to the B&B because she has to see judge, and he's not in until Monday."

"But it's Saturday," I say like an idiot.

"Exactly. Welcome to Christmas, Wyoming. I do hope you're enjoying your stay." He crosses his arms, and my head falls forward, and I massage the bridge of my nose.

So much for getting home for Christmas.

Chapter Fifteen

TRE

O utside the police station, I pull out my phone, pulling up my family chat. It's cold as fuck here, but I can't stand to be around Rowdy any longer. I'm afraid I might do something that will land me in a cell with Tessa.

> Me: I'm going to be late.

Mom: What happened now?

Lil'Sis: I'm a tad worried about your survival skills.

> Me: Good news, I won an eggnog chugging contest last night.

Lil'Sis: I don't believe it. Pics or it didn't happen.

Mom: Okay…

Me: The car got towed overnight.

Lil'Bro: It's a rental, leave it.

Me: The other driver was arrested after spouting off at the cops.

Lil'Sis: I love this woman. Tell me you're bringing her to Christmas.

Me: She has her own plans.

Something bristles inside me when I type the words and think of what Tessa might be doing with another man to ring in this Christmas season.

Lil'Bro: Leave her and come home. It's sugar cookie day today.

Mom: Sugar cookie day can wait.

Lil'Bro: MOM!

Mom: Stop acting like a four-year-old.

Me: Sorry guys.

Dad: We all understand. It's admirable of you to make sure this woman gets to where she's going. Unlike your brother.

Mom: Dad is right. It will make it all worthwhile once you get here. But hurry.

Me: I'm trying. I promise.

My phone dings with another text that I ignore for the time being.

Mom: We love you and stay safe.

Me: Love you too.

I go to my messages to see who just texted me, and it's my little sister.

Lil'Sis: What's she like?

Me: Who?

Lil'Sis: The girl, dummy.

Me: She's not a girl.

Lil'Sis: Stop deflecting.

Me: She's nice.

Lil'Sis: Smart-mouthed though?

ME: SHE'S JUST NOT EMBARRASSED TO
SPEAK HER MIND.

Lil'Sis: She sounds like someone you need in your life.

Me: I gotta go.

Lil'Sis: One day, big brother, one day it's gonna happen.

Me: Don't bet on it. Bye. See you in a few days.

Lil'Sis: You are so not fun.

Me: I'm a soldier. I'm not supposed to be fun.

Lil'Sis: That's where you're wrong. See ya.

I put my phone in my jacket pocket and look out at the small town of Christmas, Wyoming. I'm not sure I even knew the town name, but it makes the whole Jingle Balls Bed & Breakfast make more sense. Plus, there's the Reindeer Diner, Candy Cane Café, and Mistletoe Mountain Chocolatier. I love Christmas, but three hundred sixty-five days of the year, I'm not so sure about.

Walking down the stairs, I figure there's only one place to go, and that's back to see Mrs. Kringle, or whatever her real name is. The door of the bed and breakfast chimes when I open the door.

"Mrs. Kringle," I call from the front desk, hitting the little bell.

"Tre?" She comes out of the kitchen, drying her hands on a dishcloth. "You should be gone by now."

I sigh. "Tessa got arrested. Seems Rowdy isn't too happy that I won that eggnog competition."

"Oh, Rowdy Johnson. Every town has a rotten berry. He's ours."

"He said she has to see the judge, and that won't be until Monday."

She nods, understanding the predicament. "And it's Saturday..." She twists her lips for a moment. "That means Judge Sullivan is bowling at the Yuletide Lounge. You'll see Mr. Kringle over there too. If he gives you trouble, you tell him I sent you. I swear Rowdy and his crew." She shakes her head.

"Thanks. Mind if I leave our things here?" I gesture to a bench in the foyer.

She waves me off. "You two can have the same room."

"We have to leave right after I spring her, so I'll just leave them here if you don't mind." I step over to the bench.

"Sure thing. Good luck. I have to go put the finishing touches on my cookies for the fair tonight."

"Fair?" My head tilts.

"Oh yes. The Eggnog Festival kicks off all the Christmas activities around here. At the high school, there's a big Christmas fair with carnival games and prizes for the kids. I'd suggest you guys stay, but I know you have to get going."

I nod. "Yeah, but thanks for everything."

"You're welcome anytime." She goes back into the kitchen, and I head back out the front door.

I look up the Yuletide Lounge since I don't know where it is, but it turns out I'm only two blocks away from it, so I walk until I spot the words Yuletide Lounge burned into the wood sign. There are a few windows, but they're blocked with neon signs of Christmas trees, Santa faces, and holiday berries instead of alcohol and beer brands.

I open the door, and I'm surprised when it's not as dark as

I had prepared myself for. Since I never saw Mr. Kringle last night, I have no idea who he is.

I approach the bar and a guy about my age comes over. "We're not really open for regular folk yet. Can I help you with something?"

"Yes, I'm look—"

"Hey, wait, you're the guy who won the eggnog chug. How was that coming back up?" He laughs.

"Horrible. The cin—"

"Cinnamon. Yeah. Had to suck." He pauses, waiting for me to answer the question.

"I'm looking for the bowling alley."

A huge roar of laughter floats out of a room down the way.

"Oh, it's in there. Who are you looking for?" He points toward the entrance the noise came from.

"Judge Sullivan."

The corner of his lips twists. "I heard something 'bout Rowdy being Rowdy. Sorry about that. Judge doesn't know yet, I don't think, but word spread fast when your lady friend got arrested."

"How the hell does all this get around?" I ask.

He laughs. "Never lived in a small town obviously."

"How did you guess?"

"As soon as you volunteered for the chug, it was pretty clear. Only Little Becky has the nerve because she's not afraid of anything."

"Good to know." We must've had suckers written on our foreheads.

"Yeah." He crooks his finger to come closer, and I bend over the bar. "So, your lady friend..."

"Yeah?"

"She yours?"

My surprise has me delaying my answer. But now my

pause is too long. He's going to know I'm lying if I say yes, which I want to do so that this guy doesn't get any ideas.

"No, someone else's." The words taste bitter.

He shakes his head. "The good ones are always taken, huh?"

"Isn't that the truth." I point down the hall, nonverbally asking if it's okay if I head that way.

He nods. I head down the hall, following the noise, but when I get to the room, I'm confused by what I see. Multiple televisions are set up with men in folding chairs facing them and Wii controllers in their hands. They get up and bowl by swinging the remote. One guy must win it for the team because four elderly men are patting each other on the back and talking shit to another group of four. They all have gray hair—if they have hair—dressed in button-down shirts and slacks with dress shoes.

"You," a man says. "You the chugger?"

I nod. Isn't this great to be known as the chugger?

"I was looking for Judge Sullivan," I say, and everyone turns to the man who just won the game for his team.

"I don't work on Saturdays," he says. "Go away."

Jesus, is this guy related to Rowdy?

"Please," I say. "Just a few minutes."

He walks over to me, and though he's about four inches shorter than me, he's as intimidating as my drill sergeants in basic. "Teddy, put two minutes on your watch."

"Got it." A man from his team does a dramatic motion to press something on his watch.

Two minutes to plead my case. I can do this. I finish before the buzzer rings. As soon as I said Rowdy, the judge made a sour face that suggested he might see my side of things.

"She can't go touching police officers," he says when I'm finished.

I hold up my hands. "I know. It's just been a few long

travel days for us. We were due in Portland days ago, and things just keep happening to delay us."

He nods. "Sounds to me like something is working against you."

"Agreed." I nod.

"Let me get Teddy for a second." He pauses and then screams, "Teddy!"

I almost cover my ears even though half the room doesn't act as if they even heard him scream.

Teddy comes over, his gray hair and dark mustache a little overgrown. If I look closely enough, I can see the dye around the hair follicles. "What do you need?"

"The fair today. Is Johnny still out with the flu?" Judge Sullivan looks right at me as he's asking. I think he's trying to intimidate me.

"Still out as of this morning. And Jessie's got it too." Teddy smirks at me.

My stomach pitches, wondering what this could mean.

"Let's say I decide to go into work today, taking time out of my day off. We need a Santa and Mrs. Claus at the fair today. You up for that?"

I run a hand through my hair. "We really have to get going."

"This is a small town, and everyone has a job to do this time of year. Imagine the kids with no Santa or Mrs. Claus at the fair."

There's a long pause. Judge Sullivan looks at Teddy, and they both look at me.

At this rate, I won't be home by New Year's. "Of course, if you can go into work today, we'd happily pay back the favor and be Santa and Mrs. Claus."

"What a trooper!" Judge Sullivan pats me on the shoulder. "Well, I gotta get back to my bowling game."

"Um…" Teddy puts up his hand and shakes his head. "I'll just wait in the bar area."

I go back and sit with the bartender who wants to date Tessa, which isn't uncomfortable at all. I'd date her too if… my mind blanks for a moment. Why wouldn't I date her? Because she's traveling to meet someone else, because we're total opposites, or because I swore off relationships a long time ago? Might be worth figuring out.

Judge Sullivan finishes his game two hours later. I can only imagine how Tessa is being in jail. Had it been prison, she'd probably be in solitary confinement by now.

"Ready?" the judge asks, breezing right by me.

"Definitely." I follow him.

We walked over to the police station without speaking. Rowdy and his sidekick get out of their chairs when he walks in.

"Judge Sullivan," Rowdy says. "I told him he had to wait until Monday." He motions to me.

Judge Sullivan puts his hand in the air. "Get the woman out."

"But—" the tall one says.

"I don't want to hear it. We've already come to an arrangement."

Rowdy frowns but says nothing and disappears to the back.

"About time," I hear Tessa say. She comes out wearing an orange jumpsuit.

Judge Sullivan's head dips, and he pinches the bridge of his nose. "You put her in the jumpsuit?"

Both officers look at the floor. They must have thought they could get away with anything this weekend.

"Where are my clothes?"

The tall one picks up a brown paper bag off a nearby desk and hands it to her. She yanks it out of his hands.

"I'll deal with you two later. Miss, I'd like a word." Judge Sullivan turns on his heels and goes into a room with Tessa following right behind.

Meanwhile, those two assholes just sit there acting smug. I approach the long desk.

"You know it's funny how you can mask yourself, right? Like I didn't know you were a police officer last night." I look at Rowdy, who shrugs. "That's the thing about civilian clothes. No one knows your past. Take me, for example. An Army Ranger trained to be an expert in combat. We're the ones who enter enemy territory without them knowing. You fucked with her today because your badge gave you the means to do so. If I find out that one of you touched her or did anything that crossed a line, so help me, you better be ready for me. But the truth is, you'll never see me coming, and you should know I never miss my mark." I knock my knuckles on the desk and walk away as Tessa comes out of the room with the judge behind her.

I look at her and nod toward the door. "Let's go."

Tessa looks behind her. "Why are they so white-faced?" she whispers.

"Let's just get out of here."

We leave and head down the stairs, off on our next mission —Mr. and Mrs. Claus.

Chapter Sixteen

TESSA

W
e sit down at Reindeer Diner, every set of eyeballs in the place following us.

"This town is nice but kinda weird," I whisper across the table to Tre.

He lowers his menu. "After this whole Santa and Mrs. Claus thing, we're outta here."

"You already know what you're getting?" I ask, still perusing the menu for some diner food I haven't eaten yet on this road trip.

"Patty melt."

My eyes widen, and he chuckles. I will say the longer we're on this journey, the more he's loosening up.

"It's been a long few days, and I don't have any willpower right now. It took everything in me not to climb over that counter and beat the shit out of Rowdy and his sidekick."

"Because they delayed us another day?"

He looks at me for a long moment, holding my gaze. "No. Because I worried they did something to you. Please tell me they didn't. Were you given the privacy of changing in another room?"

I bite my lip to stop from smiling at his protectiveness. It shouldn't make me feel warm and fuzzy inside. I'm an independent woman, after all. But a man who goes rogue on those who hurt you is kind of sexy.

"Yeah, they seemed to have more hate for you. I think I was just the bait, and I played right into their damn hands. Probably wished it was you they could arrest."

"If we see them tonight, they better keep their distance."

Luckily, the waitress comes over to take our order. It's clear she knows who we are, but she's pretending she doesn't, even though she refers to everyone else in the place by name. We give her our order and sit in silence for a moment.

"Can I ask you a question?" It's clear from his tone that his question isn't of the "what's your favorite color" variety. Ever since our talk in bed last night, I'm not really up for a heavy conversation about me.

"What do you want to know?"

"The bakery. I just wondered if you went to culinary school. What kind of stuff did you bake?"

I unravel my paper napkin and place my silverware on the table rimmed in aluminum. "I did go to culinary school, but I ended up dropping out. And my vice is sugar, as you know, so I made cookies, cupcakes, cakes, any type of dessert really."

"I wish I could have tried some." He smiles.

"No, you don't," I say and shake my head. "Obviously they weren't so good that people couldn't get enough of them, or else I'd still be in business."

"There's a lot that goes into a business failing. It's not always about the product."

"Do we have to talk about me?" I practically grab the coffee pot from the waitress and pour my own cup just to distract myself when she comes by.

"Not if you don't want to. Want to ask me something?" He sips his black coffee.

"Sure. How upset are you that we're not on our way to Portland again? You must blame me." I frown, guilt settling on my shoulders.

He quickly shakes his head. "No. Not at all. It's not your fault we're still here. I wanted you to join me in the Eggnog Festival last night. I'm not sure I'm ready anyway." He blows out a long stream of air.

I tilt my head, forehead creased. "Ready for what?"

He's mastered body language, presumably from his military training, and it's hard to decipher when he's at ease or tense. It's the opposite of me. I'm pretty much an open book.

"Ready to go home. It's a lot of pressure." He stares into his coffee mug. It's the first sign I've seen of him being uncomfortable about his family. It's as though I'm hitting a vulnerable bone inside his tough-as-a-tank exterior.

"Why would there be pressure?" I honestly don't know because yeah, I felt it with my great-uncle, but I always imagined that if it were my parents, I wouldn't. That when I walked in the door, I'd just feel cared for by people who loved me unconditionally. Now I wonder if I was naïve.

"I joined the service at eighteen and cracked my mom's heart. When I decided on the Rangers, I broke it entirely. I've made her spend years worrying about me. Returning home sometimes feels stressful because they want the eighteen-year-old back, and I'm not sure I'm that guy anymore."

"People change as they get older."

"Yeah, but the military takes a boy and turns him into a man in about six weeks or less. Before the Army, I was..." He looks outside and smiles and shakes his head. "Carefree. A jokester. That's the version of me she wants to step through the door. Not the jaded, sullen introvert."

I itch to touch him and tell him he shouldn't feel that way, but I force myself to keep my hands curled around my warm mug of coffee. "From everything you've told me about your mother, it sounds like she'll just be happy you're home and safe."

He nods as if he's agreeing with me, but his facial expression says he's not so sure.

"Okay, so now you know why I'm okay dragging my feet. If I really was in a rush to get home, I would've driven us to an airport by now." He stares at me, and for some reason, I feel as if his words are weighted with... more. I just don't know what.

"Yeah, I know," I say in a soft voice.

"And you're okay stopping at every little unique thing we find? I'd think you'd be in a rush to get to your man." He sips his coffee but doesn't take his gaze from me. "Tell me about him."

All the hours we've spent together in the car, and he's never asked. Why does he want to know now? At first I did want to rush, but... I don't know. I've been thinking about Carter less and less.

"Right after the psychic reading, I would've gotten on a plane that night. It felt like time wasn't on my side. But now, I don't know. I keep wondering if everything she said was really about him or whether I'm wrong."

"You do seem impulsive," he says and shoots me an apologetic look.

I wave it off. "I am. Always have been. I'm not sure why. My parents died when I was nine, and I think it can give you the perspective that you aren't promised tomorrow, so you want to do everything, but I don't know. Maybe this is me. Maybe I would've been like this even if I didn't lose my parents."

He frowns and his blue eyes fill with sympathy. "I'm sorry about your parents."

The waitress comes by and saves me the usual awkwardness of responding to that statement. She slides our plates of food in front of us, and I snag a fry off his plate. He turns the plate so the fries are facing me, as if offering me as many as I want.

"So why are you really going across the country in search of love? A love that you already gave up on?"

I chuckle. "Why do I feel like I'm on *Dr. Phil* right now?"

"You don't have to answer anything you don't want to, but I don't know. I want to know each other better. We're on this adventure together, and shit keeps happening, and although I feel like I know *you* so well, I don't know much about your life, if that makes sense."

I do understand. I know that when Tre is hungry, he gets antsy in the car. If he's getting sleepy, he searches for snacks. He always insists on getting the gas first, then parks the car in a spot to use the bathroom, never leaving the car at the pump. He's quiet in the morning, but not in a grumpy or rude way. And he always lets me order first and lets me taste my meal first. But I know nothing about his actual daily life, his family, his work as a ranger. It's weird now that he mentions it.

"After my parents died, I went to go live with my great-uncle. I never really felt loved by him, more like a burden that was thrust upon him. He just passed away, and with him dying and burying him, it just struck me, you know? I'm the last of all my family. I have no one else. The psychic said I keep pushing people away, and she was right. I figure if I don't straighten up, I will die alone, just like she said, and just like my great-uncle. And there's no great-niece to come live with me at some point, so I'll spend my life as a third wheel to my best friend and her husband. He'll probably send a hitman to kill me off at some point just so they can be alone."

He laughs so hard he brings his napkin up to cover his mouth and his Adam's apple bobs with a big swallow. "You're young. You have a lot of years to find the perfect guy."

I shrug. "If I find another one, I have to put forth all the work on getting to know him. At least with this one, he already knows my faults."

"Which would be?" His expression looks as if he hasn't already experienced days with me in a small car.

I give him a wry look. "You already know them. I'm loud, impulsive, messy, jobless now, familyless. Do I really need to continue?"

He shakes his head. "That's where you're wrong. Being jobless isn't a characteristic of yours. Neither is being family-less. Why do you think that speaks to who you are as a person? And everyone needs an impulsive friend to push them out of their comfort zone, so they don't let life pass them by."

I give him a soft smile. "When did my grumpy carmate turn so sweet?"

He's quiet for a moment. "I really don't have an answer to that one." But the way he's looking at me makes me think he does.

We both laugh and get to eating. He finishes his entire plate and I take one of their chocolate croissants to go, eating as we walk back to Jingle Balls B&B.

As soon as the bell rings, Mrs. Kringle comes out of the kitchen to greet us. "You sprang her, huh?"

Tre knocks me with his elbow. "Yeah, but now we're Mr. and Mrs. Claus at the fair tonight."

"I heard something about that. You need to report to the high school in an hour or so. If you want to help me with the cookies, I'll drive you over there."

"That'd be great," I say.

We follow her into the kitchen, and there are tons of deco-rated sugar cookies wrapped in plastic bags. I pick one up and study it. Her piping is perfect, the colors vibrant.

"Do you mind?" I ask her.

"There's plenty. You have one too, Tre."

Tre glances at me. It's weird to have that little piece of

information between us that no one else knows, like we share a secret. "Thanks, but I'm watching my sugar intake."

I bite the cookie. If I was being judgmental, I'd say the cookie is too thick, but her icing is really good. "Delicious."

We help her pack up the rest, and Mrs. Kringle takes a basketful out to the car.

"I bet yours are better," he whispers to me.

"You have no idea what you're talking about."

He leans his hip on the counter, facing me. I'm not sure, but maybe I liked it better when we hated one another. This version of Tre makes me second-guess all the reasons I'm headed to Portland.

"Promise me something?" he says.

"What?"

"Before this is over, make me a sugar cookie?"

I laugh. "You mean our trip? When can I make you a sugar cookie? You won't even eat it anyway."

He stares at me for a moment, our eyes locking. "You have a crumb."

He brings his thumb to the corner of my lip and brushes it away. I close my eyes from the skin-to-skin contact. I should not be enjoying the way his calloused thumb feels along my skin.

"Sorry."

"No, it's okay. Thanks." My cheeks heat.

"I wish I could taste your sugar cookies. I bet they taste amazing."

"Well, New York didn't think so."

His gaze roams my face, and it's oddly intimate in this small kitchen filled with someone else's things. "New York doesn't know anything."

He picks up two baskets and goes outside to put them in the car.

I blow out a breath and knock my head on a cabinet. What the hell was that?

A couple minutes later, Tre and Mrs. Kringle walk back into the kitchen.

"We just got our costumes delivered by Teddy," Tre says.

"How do you know someone who lives here?" I ask.

"Long story." He places a garment bag on the table. It looks awfully small for two full Claus costumes. Tre unzips the front of the garment bag and pulls out two wetsuits—one that looks like Santa Claus and the other like Mrs. Claus. They remind me of those tuxedo shirts people buy, but these are clearly wetsuits. "What the—"

"What are we in for now?" I ask, but we just stare at one another, baffled.

Chapter Seventeen

On the way to the high school in Mrs. Kringle's giant vintage station wagon, I stare out the window, unable to stop beating myself up.

What the hell is wrong with me?

I wish I could taste your sugar cookies.

Could I sound like more of a fucking pervert?

But damn, watching her eat that sugar cookie, my insides were tearing apart. I hate everything she told me at the diner, which I asked for by asking her questions about her life. I should have kept her at arm's length like I had been. Our hatred could have remained. Losing parents at nine, being raised by a man she didn't feel loved by, failing at a business. Thinking that you're going to die alone? Fuck me, I'd have to be a cold bastard not to want to pour some happiness into her life.

It's one thing to make her smile. It's another to tell her you want to eat her sugar cookie.

And now we've been given two wetsuits for reasons unknown. It's clear I'll be seeing her in nothing but a skintight suit. After the way I woke up this morning, I'm gonna have to concentrate on some really horrific thoughts if I want to keep from sporting wood in my wetsuit. This should be pure torture.

Mrs. Kringle parks and we all head inside with baskets of cookies in hand.

"I don't get it. Shouldn't we be looking old or something? Why the wetsuits?" Tessa comes alongside me. I swear she smells like a Christmas cookie herself—like sugar and vanilla.

"Your guess is as good as mine." My voice comes out gruff because of my irritation with myself. Basically, I sound curt as fuck.

She scoffs. "So, we're back to that, I see."

She stomps past me and follows Mrs. Kringle into the high school.

I step inside behind them and stop in my tracks. What the fuck is this?

There are tricycles with giant candy canes lined up, a pit that looks as if it's filled with snowballs, Pin the Nose on Reindeer, an entire table of miniature gingerbread houses, and right at the end of the long hallway, I see a dunk tank being placed into position.

I hurry to catch up to Mrs. Kringle and Tessa, who are now in the gym.

"I thought this was a fair?" I ask Mrs. Kringle.

"Yes, in here it is. Out there is the Christmas Relay Race. Fastest person wins a five-hundred-dollar gift certificate to our big box store. It helps provide Christmas presents for local families down on their luck. The participants were chosen by raffle yesterday at the Eggnog Festival." She looks at both of us. "Only twenty people can participate. Things get pretty crazy as they get eliminated."

Mrs. Kringle brings us over to where we need to set up her cookies, and Tessa does a great job of arranging them on plate tiers and on the table.

146

"Come on, I'll show you what's about to happen." Mrs. Kringle waves for us to follow her, and she walks us back to the hallway where it says START with painter's tape across the floor. "To begin, you have to eat five mini gingerbread houses." She points at the table I saw. "Then you get on a tricycle and wind through the candy cane posts. When you finish there, you pin the nose on Rudolph while you're blindfolded. This is the first elimination. The top ten continue."

"They really take this seriously," I say.

She looks at me. "It's tradition, so we do it every year."

"And after the Rudolph?" Tessa asks.

I like the competitive sparkle in her eye. She and I could definitely have some fun at something like this.

"Then you have to shoot down three reindeer with the bow and fake arrows. After you've done that, you jump in the bin of snowballs made of yarn and find the key that opens the box to get your three balls to throw at the dunk tank." She smiles at us. "Where you two will be."

"You mean tanks? Plural?" Tessa asks.

Mrs. Kringle's wry smile says no she didn't.

"There's only one?" I ask.

"You both sit on it together. We rent it and can't afford two."

I look at Tessa, who's looking at me and clearly flabbergasted.

"Anywho, once they dunk you, they run two laps around the gym and ring the Christmas Bell to win."

I nod and rock back on my feet. "Sounds interesting."

"The race sounds fun. I wish I could do it."

God, I didn't realize she was so competitive. She strikes me as the type who would just sit and watch, cheering on the underdog.

"There's the judge. You two better get changed." Mrs.

Kringle points us in the direction of the bathrooms. "Car's unlocked."

"I'll grab the garment bag. You stay here and keep warm." I don't wait for a response from Tessa, heading back out into the parking lot to retrieve the wetsuits we have to wear.

When I return to the building, Tessa is waiting for me at the door.

"I can't believe we have to do this," she says. "I've never heard of anything like this."

"It's a kind of cool thing to do to help the families in need but make it more of a competition instead of just a handout."

We reach the bathrooms where girls are one way and boys the other.

"See you soon." I waggle my eyebrows.

"Thank God I've barely been eating on this road trip." She giggles.

She disappears into the bathroom before I can tell her how good she'd look in it either way, which is a good thing. Because I am not her boyfriend. I am not the man she's on a mission to reconnect with, and I am not the one responsible for boosting her self-esteem. I better remember that.

* * *

I walk out of the bathroom wearing my wetsuit. I assume Johnny must be about twenty pounds lighter than me because it's tight as hell. As I wait for Tessa to come out, a woman walks by me and stops. She's wearing red sparkle heels, skintight red sequin pants, and a white puffy sweater with the word Naughty stitched in red across her breasts. She's probably about twenty years older than me, but she definitely keeps herself in shape.

"You're not Johnny," she says in a coy voice.

"No, I'm not," I say.

She breaks the distance between us. "Johnny definitely doesn't fill that suit like you do." She touches my arm, and I slide over. It's clear she's been drinking, and her lipstick is smeared along the side of her mouth.

"He's sick, I heard."

"Huh..." Her gaze roams up and down my body slowly. "Can't wait to see you all wet. I bet it's impressive." She thrusts out her breasts. "I'm naughty."

"Nice to meet you, Naughty," I say and dip my head.

She giggles, but not a real one like Tessa did a few minutes ago. This woman's is fake and forced because she thinks I want her to laugh at my lame jokes when in reality, I'd prefer her to say how bad the joke was. That's what Tessa would have told me.

Jesus, can she get the hell out of my head for a fucking minute?

Speaking of, I catch a brief view of her standing outside the bathroom.

I slide out from around the woman. "Tessa."

She looks at the woman and back at me. "I don't want to interrupt."

I step forward, grab her hand, and pull her to me. "You'd never interrupt, baby." I kiss her temple and wrap my arms around her, ignoring that it feels right to have her there. "Let's go. See you later," I say to the woman who's now looking at me with disgust.

"Who was your friend, and why did you kiss me?" Tessa asks once we're far enough away. Thankfully she didn't knee me in the nuts or get pissed off because I used her for a second to escape that woman.

"She referred to herself as Naughty and told me she couldn't wait to see me wet."

Tessa glances over her shoulder then busts out laughing—

bending over at the waist, putting up her finger to give her a second.

"Your face was the best," she says once she composes herself.

"Thanks for saving me," I say dryly.

"Anytime, GI Joe. But what do you do when you're all alone?"

"I don't get hit on that much." I shrug.

She stops, and her forehead wrinkles with suspicion. "Whatever."

"Truth."

She looks me over and huffs. "Maybe it's the chip."

"What chip?"

"That chip on your shoulder. You had a pretty major one when I met you on the plane."

I chuckle. "I'm sorry, I did. What about you claiming I wasn't really in the military?"

She laughs. "God, it seems like ages ago." She walks again. "I feel like I've known you way longer than I have. It's going to be weird parting ways when we get to Portland, isn't it?" She stops talking abruptly and glances at me. I can feel her tension, waiting for my reaction.

"Agreed. It will be weird. I'll have to detox from people dragging me around giant gingerbread houses and Eggnog Festivals."

She hits me with her shoulder. "Admit it, this is something you'll remember forever." It's one of the rare times I've seen her eyes pure and clear without any turmoil in them.

"Guilty as charged."

We smile at each other, and I can't turn away from her. The air between us seems to grow thick as if there's some invisible force drawing us together.

Until someone screams my name. "Santa!"

I drag my gaze from her and turn and raise my hand. "Here."

"Good and you brought the missus," Judge Sullivan says as he approaches.

"Hi, Judge," Tessa says, lifting her hand in a small wave.

"Climb on in. We're about to start." He signals to the dunk tank.

"Convenient of you to not give me the specifics on this."

I walk toward the tank with Tessa in front of me. I deserve a Medal of Honor for not staring at her ass while she climbs the small ladder and positions herself on the small platform. I get situated beside her. Because there's not much room, we're hip to hip, thigh to thigh. I watch her chest rise and fall as she watches the starting line.

A woman comes up and hands me a beard, mustache, and a Santa hat that's going to be ruined the first time I go in. Tessa is handed a wig with a red cap stitched on top.

"I have to say, this is something we'll probably never do again," I say.

She turns to me and laughs.

"What?"

"You're just a little skewed." She fixes my hat and beard. Even her knuckles are soft as they run down my cheeks, positioning the beard just so. "There you go."

"Thanks."

Her tongue slides along her lips. "Anytime."

Bullhorns go off, which must mean the race is starting. It's organized chaos, families following their loved ones from station to station. Faster than I was prepared for, some competitors are at the tank, armed with balls. The man in first place is a large guy with big muscles, and Tessa grabs my hand, obviously preparing to take the plunge.

"I'm sure the first time will be the worst," I try to reassure her, but I don't know if it helps at all.

The man misses with every shot, so he has to go back to the snowball pit and get another key. Meanwhile, another guy comes over with balls in hand. He's thinner than the other guy. The first ball he throws is close and Tessa screams.

I laugh because we weren't dunked, and Tessa is clutching me as though we're going to be dropped into a vat of acid. When he throws his second ball, he hits the target. The board drops, depositing us into the tank. The cold water makes my lungs seize for a moment, and my hat and beard fly off. I stand immediately, waiting for Tessa.

She pops up, laughing hysterically. "Oh my god, that was so fun. But I'm not sure I can get back on the board. Can you help me?"

I place my hands on her hips, our bodies so close I'd only have to take one step forward, and we'd be flush. I lift her, and she climbs on the board, but I don't want to get up because I now have a chub. Which I can't fucking hide in this damn wetsuit.

"Let's go, Santa. People are waiting," one of the organizers yells.

I climb back up, looking like a horny adolescent boy. Tessa glances down and inhales a deep breath.

"It's a natural response to having your hands on a woman."

She shakes her head. "I wouldn't think anything else."

And then the big guy is back again and dunks us back in the water. The cold water helps to keep it down.

By the time it's over, we're dunked eight times, and the first guy rings the Christmas Bell as the winner.

After we get dressed and hand back the wetsuits to the judge, he gives us our car keys. "It's outside in the parking lot. Thank you both. Small towns depend on a lot of help from their residents, and we appreciate you guys delaying your trip."

"It was a lot of fun," Tessa says.

The judge gives her a smile. "Here's a basket of items to take with you to remember Christmas, Wyoming. We do hope you'll come visit again."

The basket is full of baked goods from the different vendors at the fair.

"Thanks," we say in unison.

As if either of us is ever going to see each other again once this road trip is complete. It's a one-and-done.

Chapter Eighteen

TESSA

After picking up our stuff from Jingle Balls Bed & Breakfast, we're back in the car and on our way. Tre is driving this leg of the trip, and we're headed back to the highway.

I watch the snow-covered ground pass by and look at the mountains in the distance. "I'm going to miss it in a way."

His head whips my way. "Why?"

Isn't it obvious to him? Then again, he has a family. "They're all there for one another. Sure, it's a little weird and I've never lived in a small town where people know your business, but it's nice how they all look out for one another."

He merges and slows for a truck that's barreling down the highway. "I get what you're saying. I can see how you'd like that. But you do know that family doesn't have to be blood, right?"

I stare out the window again. Dusk is descending faster than I thought. Pretty soon it will be dark. "Yeah, my best friend, Kenzie, says the same thing."

"Exactly. You have her and her husband as your family. Sometimes families don't even get along. I mean, my mom doesn't really talk to her extended family anymore. There was a falling out, and we don't celebrate holidays with them anymore. We make separate arrangements to see my grandparents so we don't have to be with my aunt, uncle, and cousins during the holidays."

I look away from the window and back at him. "If I ever get married, I hope my husband comes from a big family. And then I want to make a big family."

He raises his eyebrows. "So Boy Wonder comes from a big family?"

I frown. "You know what, I don't really know. He'd talk about his family quite a bit, but he was really more about his career. I never got the details. Then again, it wasn't that many dates. How much can you find out about a person in three dates?"

He glances over, turns on the signal, and gets in the fast lane to pass someone. "I know a lot about you, and it's only been, like, four days."

Tre's been acting a little different lately, not so distant, and I kind of like it. As if we might actually be friends after this. "It's four days straight, and we're together all the time."

"Except for your stint in jail." He laughs.

I don't. "Not my finest moment. I'm not sure I ever said thank you, by the way."

"You don't need to. It was wrong what they did in the first place."

"Maybe, but I was a little out of line. And you didn't leave me. That meant a lot."

"Leave no man behind," he says and smirks.

But what does that smirk mean? Does he see me as another soldier? Sometimes this whole trip feels like a mission, and we're never going to reach Portland. Is he starting to feel the same thing I am in the pit of my stomach, or is it just that we're becoming friends? Allies instead of enemies. I wish I knew.

"Well, it's been a pleasure serving with you these past few days," I say.

He shakes his head, but the edges of his lips are tipped up. It's his classic "I find you amusing, but I'm trying not to show it" face. It's by far his sexiest look, and if I'm honest, it makes me want to lean over and kiss him.

I situate myself in my seat and eventually must fall asleep because when I wake up, it's dark outside, but the car is so hot you'd think there was a fire in here.

"Shit," I say and sit up in my seat. Grabbing the hem of my sweater, I tear it off. "What's going on?"

Tre has stopped the car on the side of the highway and is fiddling with the knobs. "I have no idea. It started, like, five miles back. I went to turn it down, but I mistakenly turned it higher, and now the cooling button isn't working." His finger keeps pressing and pressing, but nothing happens.

I look at the road and a semi-truck's lights coming up behind us shine on the sign in front of us. Helena, Montana, is only ten miles away. "Maybe we can find another rental place and switch out the car?"

Tre gives me a look as though he thinks I'm delusional and naive, but what choice do we have? He grabs his sweatshirt and pulls it off his body, tossing it with mine in the back. He's wearing another army T-shirt, and of course, it fits him perfectly, showing off his biceps and his strong shoulders. My body buzzes with awareness.

"Is Army stuff the only clothes you own?" I ask.

He puts his seat belt back on and eases the car back onto the highway. "Well, it's a major part of my life."

I nod. "I guess I can see that." I imagine what he would look like in a suit. I bet he'd be mouthwateringly hot.

"What did you wear to the bakery?" he asks.

"An apron."

He glances at me, and I swear his gaze dips to my breasts. His teeth bite his bottom lip, and I squirm in my seat, wishing I could read his mind. "Is that all?"

I laugh and shove his shoulder. "No, usually jeans and a T-shirt with the bakery name on it too."

"Which was?"

"Happy Treat." There's a pinch in my chest when the words leave my mouth.

"I like it," he says, but what else would he say?

"Well, no one else did apparently." I roll down my window, unable to take the heat anymore, and the cold air blasts inside. "I can't take it. I'm sweating."

"If you want to take off another layer, I understand."

My head rears back at his flirtatious comment. "Look who's coming out of his shell."

"I was joking."

I shrug. "Okay then." I'm not sure I believe him.

He looks me over. "I would never," he says with concern in his tone that I didn't take it as a joke.

"Relax, it's not a big deal." *I kind of liked it* is what I don't have the courage to say.

He pulls off at the exit to Helena. I grab my phone, searching for a rental place. Maybe our luck is changing because there's one only a couple of miles ahead, and they're actually open.

When we pull up in front of the rental car place, we look at one another. There's got to be some hitch because nothing has gone smoothly for us so far.

He turns off the car, and we grab our sweater and sweat-shirt, put them on, and rush inside to get out of the cold. The bell chimes, and Christmas carols ring out from the overhead speakers. Garland with silver berries is wrapped around the edge of the counter where an employee stands.

The woman behind the counter stares at us the entire way from the door to the counter. "I have no cars."

"We have a car of yours to return. The heat won't turn down," Tre says.

She leans to the side to have a look through the windows behind us and straightens again. She's probably in her midfifties or so and is just getting some gray hair sprinkled in her dark strands. She blows out a breath.

"Like I said, we don't have any other cars. If you want to leave it here, you can though. Our guy will look at it, and if it was your fault, you'll be charged."

Tre's eyes narrow at her. "Believe me, it's not our fault. You think we want to be out a car three days before Christmas?"

"Well, I don't have anything for you." She shrugs.

"Do you know when a car is expected to be returned?" Tre asks as dignified and polite as he always is.

She never looks at her computer or any paperwork. "Nope."

"Do you know anything?" he asks, his voice rising for the first time I've ever seen.

We're coming to his breaking point, I think, so I slide in to take over and give him a break. "What do you suggest we do then? Is there another car place around?"

"Listen, lady"—her eyes flick to Tre for a moment and come back to me—"you're obviously aware it's three days before Christmas. There's nothing I can do. Do you think this is a treat for me to sit here and tell people one after the other that there's nothing I can do for them? But the company demands I stay open on the off chance someone brings a car back. This job isn't a picnic."

I lean forward and she gives me a death glare, but I don't step back. "We've been traveling for four days from

Minnesota, and we're exhausted. Let's just say our trip hasn't been easy. Surely there's something you can do."

She blows out a breath. "The only thing I can tell you is there's a train station about four blocks to the north. That's about your only choice if you want to get out of town soon. As far as a rental car, it's not an option."

I turn around and look at Tre. He blows out a breath and palms the back of his neck, but needless to say, we both know we have no choice.

"We'll leave the car here then, but the heat isn't our fault," Tre says.

She nods. "I'll tell management." She holds out her hand, and Tre places the keys in her palm.

"Just let us get our stuff." I walk out, and right before I leave, I turn. "Merry Christmas. Thank you."

"I hope you get home in time for Christmas," she says, her attitude changing.

We grab all our stuff out of the vehicle, and I look up which way we have to head to the train station. Tre takes my suitcase to pull behind him while carrying his duffel in his other hand.

"I can take my own bag," I say, reaching for the handle.

He moves the bag away from me. "I got it."

"Why? I can do it."

"I know you can do it. I'm being nice." He flashes me a smile that would make most women's panties dissolve on the spot.

"Why?"

"Oh, am I not nice?" He starts walking, and I follow.

"No, you are, but it's just, I don't know..." It feels like something a boyfriend does for you.

"Good, then just let me, no complaints." He winks. I've figured out in the short time we've been together that it's his signature move to say he's joking.

We walk four blocks, and by the time we reach the train station, my hands feel numb and every part of my body is freezing.

"What the hell?" Tre mumbles as we weave between people to get to the line to buy a ticket. It's really busy.

"I hope they're all going east," I say, looking at all the families. Travel isn't easy during the holidays and next year, I think my ass will be on my couch.

"Same."

While we wait in line, we search on our phones and figure out that there's a train leaving in half an hour, but with how slow the line is moving and with all the people here, I'm not sure if we can get tickets to be on it. Finally, we're at the front of the line.

"Two to Portland," Tre says.

"Sure thing. You guys got the last two," the ticket agent says.

Tre slides his credit card over. "Something finally goes our way," he says to me.

"I'll pay you back," I tell him for the millionth time.

Tre ignores my words. "It's packed tonight. Holidays, huh?"

"That and there're issues at the airport. People are trying to find alternate ways to get where they're going." The agent shakes his head. "And here you two go."

He slides the tickets over, and Tre takes them, putting them in his pocket. "Thanks."

"You're welcome. Enjoy your ride."

"I think we will as long as we can sleep," I say, and he chuckles.

We stand on the platform, waiting for the train to arrive. There's not a lot of space, and I'm pressed right into Tre. He keeps all our belongings wedged in front of us, his arm protectively placed so no one can bump us. I look up at the dark stubble on his chin and jawline that's grown in over the past few days.

He looks down at me and smiles. "What?"

"Nothing. Just going over the last few days in my mind." I don't tell him how safe he makes me feel, even when he's doing hardly anything. Like right now, the position of his arm and the way he has our bags. It's just second nature to him. He's a protector.

"Crazy, right?"

"I'm not sure I would have survived without you," I say.

He chuckles. "Oh, you would have. Give yourself some credit."

But he's wrong. I owe him so much more than the money he's spent to get us this far. "No, you carried me."

"Well, you've made this trip entertaining and memorable."

Our eyes connect and neither of us looks away.

It's way too intense, so I blink and shift my focus. "Thanks," I say, but not directly to him.

He doesn't say anything. When the train arrives, we don't rush on like the others, but take our time. When we find our seats, Tre demands that I sit by the window, and he takes the aisle.

"Let's cross our fingers that this is our last leg." I hold up my crossed fingers.

"Let's hope so," he says.

The train leaves the station and as excited as I should be, there's a giant pit in my stomach too, because I realize that I don't want my time with Tre to end.

Chapter Nineteen

TRE

The train has only been rolling for about an hour, and surprisingly, neither of us has fallen asleep. Being around people feels a little weird since it's been only us two in the car.

I roll over what I want to ask her a few times before I decide to just go for it. "Can I ask you a favor?"

She turns in her seat to face me. "Anything. I mean, after all you've done for me."

She's so hung up on the money aspect of the trip, while I've barely given it much thought.

"I haven't bought my family anything yet. I'd planned to do it when I arrived in Portland, what was supposed to be days ago. I was thinking we'd stay in Portland for the day when we get there, and maybe you could help me pick out some gifts for them. I know you're eager to meet up with—"

"Oh no." She grabs my hand. "I'd love to help you."

"Great. Do you know where you're going after we split up?"

She shakes her head. "I haven't messaged him yet. The

nerves are really settling in right now. Am I a complete lunatic for doing this?"

"Honestly, when you first said it, I did find it strange, but now..." I shake my head. "I don't."

She pokes my side. "Are you saying that you're a believer in love now?"

I huff. "Far from it, but I'm not so sure I'd be upset if you showed up at my door."

She smiles, one that I've already committed to memory. It's her smile where she feels complimented, flattered, and appreciated. I could get used to waking up to that smile every morning.

"Thanks for saying that," she says.

I open my mouth to tell her how serious I am but shut it. I'm not going to ambush her journey, especially when I don't really know for certain what I want.

She leans her head back on the comfy seat and turns her head to look at me. "Was it a girl?"

I'd grabbed a magazine at the gas station on our last stop and put it in the pocket of the seat in front of me, so I grab it now. "A girl?"

"I just wondered if you don't believe in love because you experienced heartache at some point."

I chuckle and shake my head. "Interested in dissecting me, huh?"

"You don't have to tell me, but I figured we have some time." She sits up straighter, slips off her shoes, and crosses her legs, facing me sideways in the seat.

"It's a long story..."

She places her chin in her palm. "Whenever you're ready."

I look around the train for a moment before I decide that I have nothing to lose in telling her—at least part of it. "Well, when I went to basic, I was single, but most guys in my bunkhouse weren't. They call them Dear John letters, as you probably know. It didn't take a week before some of my bunk-mates were receiving them from girlfriends they thought they'd marry. One after the other, the letters would come after weeks of unanswered calls or letters. It's worse when we're out on missions to see guys get them."

"Oh, that's hard," she says. "But it didn't happen to you?"

"No, but I was smart enough not to date someone before going in, and I haven't pursued a serious relationship since." There's more I'm not telling her, but I'm not going to get into the reason for that right now. "I have a job that's hard to cut off, leave at work, so I've always closed myself off to love. It's hard to think I can trust someone after seeing all those girls crying their eyes out, saying goodbye to their boyfriend, fiancé, or husband, and it would all just change after they were deployed."

"So, until you retire from the military, you're going to refrain from falling in love? It's not really a choice, you know."

I laugh to myself. "As long as I don't put myself in the position to fall in love, I won't."

She rocks her head back. "Good luck with that."

"You don't believe me."

She shrugs. "No, I just think it's not something you can always control. You're acting as if your heart is a brain. That it can weigh pros and cons. A heart beats, it feels."

"A heart is an organ," I remind her, and her mouth hangs open in mock shock.

How can someone who has had shit thrown her way since her parents died at nine still be such a big believer in love?

"Says a man who has never been in love."

"And you have?" I ask. She has a point. I've never allowed myself to open up and feel that strongly for someone. Actually, Tessa's the first person I've ever felt this desire to grow closer to, and I'm sure it's only because we were thrown together in unusual circumstances and I've spent so much time with her. Usually, I like one night, maybe two, but that's where it ends.

She shrugs. "I'm not sure, but at least I'm open to it."

"And this guy in Portland? You think he might be the one?" There's an edge to my tone, and from the way her head tilts, she hears it.

"I honestly don't know, but I'm going to try and see. All I know is that I want to spend my life with someone, and I hope that one day every love song on the radio makes sense, and every romantic comedy confirms that my heart is right. Most of all, I hope I fall hard, and if it breaks me, if *he* breaks me, at least I'll know I didn't give up. I just can't help but think that after all the shit I've been through, I'm meant to find where I belong, and when I do, I'll do everything I can not to fuck it up."

I stare at her for a moment. This beautiful baker from New York is a hell of a lot braver than I am.

"I don't really expect you to understand." She turns to stare out the window, but since it's dark outside, all we can see is our own reflections in the glass.

"Well, who knows? Maybe one day I will."

I bury my head in the magazine, and she stares out the window, curling up in the seat with her jacket over her like a blanket. At some point, she closes her eyes and relaxes.

I blow out a breath and admire her. Her heart is so open and welcoming. But we're such different people. She must sense my eyes on her because she opens hers, a soft smile forming across her lips.

"Is something wrong?" she whispers since most of the passengers are asleep.

"No." I shake my head.

"Then what is it?"

I'm not sure I can be honest with her, but there is something I need to tell her. "I know I should regret not giving you the first-class seat, but I don't."

"No?" she asks with amusement, eyes still sleepy.

"No. I'm glad we became friends, and we wouldn't have if you hadn't sat beside Polly, and if she hadn't had her baby on the plane, and if my license wasn't expired and your credit card wasn't declined. Maybe I'm just really tired and rambling." I push a hand through my close-cropped hair.

She takes my hand and shifts in her seat, grabbing her phone. "Cause and effect. Or maybe fate, who knows, but we have to exchange numbers, you know, now that we're friends." There's a sparkle in her blue eyes that I don't want to read into. We exchange phone numbers, then she leans her head on my shoulder. "Just so you know, friends use each other's shoulders to sleep on."

The smell of the holiday berries shampoo from Jingle Bells B&B floats around us, but I close my eyes, and soon sleep takes both of us.

* * *

I'm already awake when the train conductor announces that the next stop is Portland. Tessa's head has been on my shoulder the entire time and my mind has played havoc on me since I awoke. What is this feeling inside me?

Why do I wish we could have more delays so I can spend more time with her?

"Tessa," I whisper. "We're here."

She squirms and stretches her arms, hitting me in the face. "Oh, sorry," she says, her cheeks turning the sweetest shade of pink. "We're really in Portland?"

"We are. I guess you need to call your friend." I'm not sure why I decide that's the first thing I should bring up.

"No, we're shopping, remember?" She smiles at me, still a little sleepy and cute as hell.

"Right."

The train stops and we file out, grabbing our bags like we're a real couple, each one knowing the movements of the other. She knows I'll wait outside the aisle, let her file out first and follow behind. She rushes ahead of me and waits at the bags as I knew she would as if I don't know what both of our bags look like at this point.

I've never once had this in my life, and I'm surprised that I'm kind of enjoying it.

"Let's go shopping," she says, excitement filling her tone. I groan and she laughs. "What is it with men and shopping?"

She's not looking for an answer from me, and that's what I like the most.

I call us a taxi, and we head to the mall in downtown Portland. I wish I could concentrate on anything but her and the fact she's going to be meeting up with that douchebag any time now, while I'll go home to my parents and try to push her out of my head.

Jesus, where did this heartburn come from?

"Are you okay?" she asks in the back of the cab.

"Yeah, why?"

"You're rubbing your chest." She mimics my behavior, and I look down to see my hand over my heart.

"Just some heartburn. All the junk food. My body isn't used to it."

She's quiet for a moment. "Let's eat first then. Get something decent in you."

When the cab ride is finished, we find a nearby restaurant and head in. To my surprise, my name is called a few seconds after we walk in and I'm shocked when I see who it is.

"Tre?" Callie says as if she's not sure it's really me.

I feel Tessa stiffen next to me.

"Callie?" I think I might frown.

"Like you could ever forget me." She swats at my chest and her eyes take in Tessa next to me. "Who's this?"

Without thinking, I wrap my arm around Tessa's shoulders, pulling her into my side. "This is my girlfriend, Tessa."

"Oh," Callie says with a small frown.

Tessa pinches my back, and I pretend it didn't hurt.

Callie puts out her perfectly manicured hand. "Pleasure to meet you."

Tessa shakes her hand, still a little tense.

"I just ran into your mom last week, and she said nothing about a girlfriend."

"I'm surprising them," I lie, earning another pinch.

"She'll love that. I feel like maybe I should vet you." She looks Tessa up and down with a strained laugh.

I'm surprised Tessa has been so quiet thus far.

"Well, it was nice seeing you. We're going to eat. Merry Christmas and tell your family I said the same." I smile and walk to the hostess stand.

"I've got time. I'll join you. We can catch up." Callie comes up alongside me. "Three, please."

"You're not here with anyone?" Tessa asks.

"No. I wasn't lucky enough to snag a guy like Tre here. Everyone in town is going to be crying tonight." Now her gaze roams up and down my body as though she wants to undress me.

Callie and I hung around the same crowd in high school, and we were pretty good friends, but she always made her interest in me very apparent.

Tessa steps in closer to me. "Yeah, we're both really lucky." There she goes, pinching me again.

"I'm the lucky one." I look down at Tessa.

Our eyes catch and maybe she's just playing along, but I swear for a moment, something passes between us.

The hostess seats us at a round booth and somehow I end up in the middle of the two women. I made a mistake saying Tessa was my girlfriend, but Callie is a stage five clinger. If she found out I was in town and single, she'd be climbing the terrace of my parents' house and I'd probably find her naked in my childhood bed. It happened twice in high school.

All I can hope for now is that Tessa plays along. One meal and we'll go shopping, and Callie will continue on her way.

"So, Tessa, tell me your meet-cute," Callie says after the waitress takes our order.

Tessa looks at me and smirks. Oh fuck, what is she going to say?

Chapter Twenty

TESSA

Why do I feel competitive with Callie? Tre isn't mine, even if he's trusting me to pretend to be his girlfriend. I should be on my way to Carter by now, but when Tre asked me to go shopping with him, it was a no-brainer. And that's when it hit me—I'd rather shop with him than go find Carter. More and more, something is tugging me to stay here with him, and I'm trying to ignore it, but I'm not sure how much longer I can.

"Our meet-cute?" I ask, only to buy myself some time and not because I don't know what a meet-cute is. Every self-respecting romance reader knows what a meet-cute is.

"You know. How you guys met, got together?" She smiles. Her nails are perfectly manicured, her makeup flawless, and I'd bet that her outfit costs more than my entire wardrobe. I can't help but wonder how she's seeing me. Lacking, I'm sure.

In the last four days, I haven't done my makeup, and my clothes are wrinkly from being jammed in a suitcase the majority of the time. And after the long train ride, I'm in desperate need of a shower.

"Oh." I look at Tre and laugh, and his eyebrows shoot up.

I could toss this his way and put him in the hot seat. But I slide a little closer to him in the booth and place my hand on his thigh. His leg jolts but calms down right away, hopefully not giving away that us touching each other is a foreign concept. "We met on a plane."

Tre inhales and exhales, doing his best to appear relaxed, but he looks a little tense, probably wondering what the hell I'm going to say. But he has nothing to fear because I'm just going to give her the truth—or a version of it.

"I was in my first-class seat, and Tre approached me and said it was his seat. Of course, he was dressed in his fatigues, looking like the ideal hot military guy. Every woman around was drooling, especially the one next to me. The flight attendant got involved and turns out there was a mix-up and we were assigned the same seat."

"I swear, airlines." Callie dips a chip into the salsa and eats it.

"I got up and gave Tre the first-class seat because he's military and deserves to have it over me. He does so much for our country."

"Really?" Callie asks.

"Yep. And then we got to baggage claim, and he thanked me for the seat, asked me out to dinner to repay me, and the rest is history." I squeeze his thigh and smile widely at him.

"That's kind of romantic, I guess." Callie dips another chip in.

"Well, you know Tre, he wasn't looking for a girlfriend."

"Oh, I know. The girls from our hometown have been chasing him forever."

That doesn't come as any surprise to me. Who wouldn't want a man who's as hot as he is, plus caring and protective?

The waitress comes over and Callie orders a margarita with an extra shot of tequila, Tre orders a water, and I order a diet soda.

172

"Tell me about yourself, Tessa. You must live in Georgia too?"

I stare at her for a moment, trying to wrap my head around what she just said. Georgia? But he took a flight from New York. I guess that could have been a connection, but how did I never even ask where he lives? And what is this disappointment squeezing my chest now that I know we don't live in the same area? I mean, it's not as if I thought we'd be spending time together back in New York, right?

"Actually," I say, but Tre puts his hand over mine to stop me.

Sure, he can take this one.

"We're doing long distance right now. With me retiring and all, I didn't want her to uproot her life in New York City."

"New York City?" This is the first time Callie's looked impressed, as if everyone who lives in New York City is wealthy. Probably just the parts she knows about.

I could tell her a story or two about the down-on-their-luck people. The people who work their asses off to make a modest life for their families. Something tells me that Callie lives in a world where she only sees what she wants to though, and if confronted by reality, she wouldn't see it anyway.

But as she gets hung up on the big city I'm from, I'm still processing the word *retiring*. Did Tre really just say he's retiring from the military? Why do I feel slighted that he didn't tell me in the four days we were together, but Callie across from me finds out at the same time I do?

"I love New York City," Callie says, elongating every letter. "The shopping, the food, the theater."

I nod.

The waitress brings our drinks and Callie asks her something, so I use it as my opportunity to poke Tre in the leg. He rears back as if I hurt him and looks at me.

I mouth, *Retiring?*

He just shakes his head. Does that mean he isn't retiring, or does that mean we can't talk about it right now? A large part of my brain is saying, *Why do you care? You're about to part ways with this man in mere hours.*

"They try to make the drinks so weak nowadays." Callie shakes her head. "I don't like drinking alone."

"Well, we just got in. Time change." Tre shrugs.

The waitress comes back with another drink for Callie, and I glance at Tre. I understand now why I'm sitting next to him pretending to be his girlfriend. She strikes me as someone who doesn't understand the word no. I cannot picture Tre being with a woman like this.

We place our food order with the waitress, and she leaves us to our conversation again.

"I ran into your mom. She was at the grocery store, buying all your faves." Callie smiles with the straw between her lips.

Tre tenses under my hand. "Yeah, she's really excited."

"As she should be. You know you've always been her favorite." Callie looks at me. "Tre was babied."

"No, I wasn't." He shakes his head, leaning back into the booth for the first time. "I'm just the one who left her first."

"Tell me about you," I say because I don't want Callie to hammer more questions at us, and even though I want to hear about Tre's life, I don't really want to hear it from this woman. It sours the whole experience.

"Me? Well, I'm single." She holds up her left hand. "And I had been waiting on this guy until he showed up with you on his arm."

I choke on my diet soda but manage to swallow it down. Do I say I'm sorry?

Tre puts his arm around my shoulders, pulling me in and kissing the top of my head. I sink into the strength of his body. "You know we were always just friends, Callie."

Callie studies us, and I see her jealousy light up her green eyes. "You put me in the friend zone."

I bite the inside of my cheek. This is awkward.

"You know what? I'm going to go to the bathroom. I'll be right back." I slide out.

Tre's hand grazes across my back and down my arm until he secures my hand. He tightens his hand on mine. Leaning toward me, it's clear what he's about to do, and I freeze. Is he joking?

His lips land on mine in a chaste kiss, and I shut my eyes at his soft but firm lips. My body buzzes as he pulls away.

"Hurry back," he whispers, releasing me.

Now you leave, Tessa.

My brain knows what to do, but my body says let's do that again. Somehow I force myself to slide out of the booth and walk to the bathroom, touching my lips the entire time. I can't get my phone out fast enough once I'm inside.

Come on, Kenzie, answer the phone.

"Well look who has graced me with a call?" Kenzie says.

"Okay, save it. I don't have much time, and I'm in crisis."

She laughs.

"I'm serious. I'm in Portland."

"Oh, did something happen with Carter? Does he not want you to come visit?"

"What? No. I haven't even called him yet." I wave off her assumption even though she can't see me.

"Okay... so what's the crisis?"

"I'm at the mall helping Tre pick out gifts for his family, and we ran into some old high school friend of his. He told her I was his girlfriend, and he just kissed me on the lips. No tongue or anything, but oh man. I'm going to remember that kiss for the rest of my life. I just know it."

Dead silence.

"Kenz?" I hold my phone out for a moment to make sure

the call didn't drop, but no, we're still connected. I bring the phone back to my ear.

"I had a feeling this was going to happen," she says.

"What?"

"Can I ask you why, when you got to Portland after being delayed for days, did you not call Carter right away? He's the whole reason you went there. Instead, you decide to go shopping with this Tre guy?"

I know the answer, but admitting it out loud would make it real, and if what I think is happening is really happening, then I've put myself in a position for heartbreak.

"Yeah, you don't have to answer me. I've known since the last time you called me." She must be doing something on her computer because I hear typing in the background.

"Known what?"

"I'm not gonna tell you because you already know."

Jeez, she sounds about as vague as that damn psychic. "How do you know I know?" My voice grows louder from my defensiveness.

"Because I know you. You don't want to admit it to yourself because if you do, then it's real. If you think it's part of your imagination, then you can't get hurt."

My eyebrows draw down in my annoyance. "You're choosing now to psychoanalyze me?"

More typing.

"I want you to think of the real reason you went across the country for Carter," she says.

"Because I thought he was the one."

"*The* one or the one the psychic was talking about?"

"Both."

"And maybe this guy, the military one, is who you were really supposed to meet. Maybe he's the reason you were supposed to head west."

I shake my head. "I cannot do this right now. You're

messing with my head."

She sighs. "Okay, just do me one favor. Don't shy away from whatever you're feeling. You followed your instincts to get you to Portland. Keep following what your gut is telling you. I guarantee it's leading you in the right way."

"This was not at all helpful. I better get back to the table before one of them comes looking for me."

"Call me with the good news," she says, and I hear the smile in her tone.

"What good news?"

"Once you sleep with him. Love you, bye." She hangs up.

I stare at the phone for a moment before putting it in my purse. I leave the bathroom and I'm walking across the restaurant when my eyes catch Tre's. There's relief in his that I'm returning.

As if he's under a spotlight, he's the only one I can see. Butterflies fill my stomach, and my body feels anxious to be next to him again. My hand wants his hand in mine. My lips want his lips on mine. I stumble a bit as I walk before I recover because it hits me—sometime in the last four days, I fell hard for him.

I think about what Kenzie said about following my gut as I slide into the booth, getting as close to Tre as I can. He places his hand on my thigh, dangerously close to where I really want his hand to be. God, this feels perfect and right, but then the words he told ring through my mind over and over again, "I don't believe in love."

My heart cracks because if I follow my gut, then I'm not going to call Carter after Tre leaves. Which means I'm going to go home alone. But I'd rather be alone than search out a guy who doesn't compare to the one sitting next to me. As if he can hear my thoughts, Tre squeezes my thigh and smiles at me like this isn't an act. I smile back because at least now, I know how love is supposed to feel.

Chapter Twenty-One

TRE

"Are you sure you don't want my help?" Callie asks outside of the restaurant, which took way too fucking long to serve us. I thought we were never gonna get out of there. Add on the fact that I made a monumental mistake when I kissed Tessa and that meal felt as if it took for fucking ever.

What the hell was I thinking?

I know what I was thinking. I've been dying to know what those lips taste like, and I used the weak excuse of her pretending to be my girlfriend to do it. It was shitty pushing her into that.

"No, we're good," I say. I take my arm from around Tessa and wrap Callie in a hug. "Merry Christmas. It was good to see you."

"You too." She's one of those tight huggers who takes your breath away. Even though I know it, it surprises me every time. She shifts from me to Tessa and tugs her into her arms. "You lucky, lucky girl." She laughs. "Watch your back when you get to Climax Cove." She laughs again then releases Tessa as though she's a rag doll. "I'm just kidding."

"Have a great holiday if I don't see you." Tessa is nothing but polite.

Finally, we say one more goodbye, and I take Tessa's hand and turn her toward the mall while Callie heads back to her car, having already finished her shopping.

"So, where do you want to go first? Who should we get?" Tessa asks.

I'm surprised she doesn't grill me with questions about Callie, or I don't know… why the hell I kissed her.

"My sister is the easiest," I say.

We turn the corner out of Callie's view and neither of us unlinks our hands. There's no reason we need to be holding hands right now, other than we want to. I know I want to, but does she?

"What does your sister like? How old is she?" Tessa walks us into some bath store and drops my hand when she reaches for a candle. "Candles?" She removes the lid and shoves it under my nose.

"She's twenty-three, and I don't really know what she likes. I haven't been home much." Seeing how much Tessa wants to be a part of a family makes me feel guilty for abandoning mine. I don't make it home as often as I should, and sometimes my excuses are lame.

"Okay." She looks around the store and beelines it over to a girl shopping with her mom. "Excuse me. How old are you?"

The girl looks at her mom. "Twenty-one," she says warily.

"Perfect. We're looking for a gift for his sister and she's twenty-three. Tell me what the hot things you want this year are."

The girl looks at me and back at Tessa. "Anything comfy, like sweatpants and cozy slippers."

The mom interrupts. "Does she live on her own?"

Tessa looks back at me.

"She's just getting her own apartment with a roommate," I say.

"Then how about something for her move?" the woman says. "Like a coffee maker, margarita maker, or even just margarita glasses."

"Jewelry!" the daughter says.

"Perfect." Tessa smiles. "Thanks." She walks back over to me. "Come on, I know the perfect gift now."

We end up buying a margarita maker and four glasses for Brynn.

"Okay, who's next? Let's do your mom last. That's tricky."

"I guess my brother then."

"How old? What's he into?"

I shrug. My brother and I are complete opposites. "He lives on his own and has everything he needs there. I'm thinking for him maybe a game remote. He's a big gamer."

"Cool, let's go."

We end up getting my brother and my dad done. Then we pick out a nice necklace for my mom with the initials of all her children. Tessa makes me buy wrapping paper and tape, not allowing me to use the gift wrapping service because she says making it look pretty is half of the heart that goes into buying a gift.

Once we're done buying all the gifts, we sort of stand there staring at each other for a beat. Is this it? Is this where we part ways? My chest aches at the thought.

"It's getting late in the day, so I think I'm going to head home tomorrow morning. I should probably book a hotel," I say. We haven't discussed her plans for calling douchebag yet. And it's only getting later now.

"Oh, okay." She pauses for a beat. "Do you want help wrapping the presents?"

Relief eases the knot in my chest that this won't be our goodbye. "I've never wrapped a gift before," I admit. And I'm telling the truth as long as you don't consider when I was younger.

"I can go with you to the hotel for a bit to help." She almost looks... hopeful.

"Are you sure?"

"Of course. It's the least I can do since I haven't been able to pay you back yet."

"You don't have to."

I pull out my phone to look up hotels with availability. Once I book a room, I order an Uber and tell Tessa the car we're looking for.

"I feel like I'm taking you away from your quest," I say because I feel as if I should, not because I want to remind her of why she's in Portland in the first place.

She laughs and shrugs. "Honestly?" She tilts her head, looking at me, and there's something in her eyes, something she's hiding. "I'm not so sure anymore." I open my mouth to respond, but she points behind me. "There's our ride."

I follow her to the Uber, and on the ride to the hotel, I try to decipher what she meant by she's not so sure anymore. What is she not sure about? I hate this feeling, anxious about the moment we're going to part ways, but also very much wanting to enjoy every last second I can with her.

The drive doesn't take too long, and we get out of the car with all our stuff, which we can barely carry. Thankfully, the bellhop gives us a cart and Tessa takes charge of putting it all on there. I go to the desk and check in.

"I've always wanted to get on one of these things and race." She pushes the luggage cart toward the elevator after I return with the room key.

I wait until we're on the elevator and it stops at our floor. "Hop on."

"Really?" She gets on the cart, sitting on her suitcase as I push her and let the cart go.

I continue to push her down the hall and she puts her arms up at one point as though she's riding a roller coaster. I try to commit her laugh to memory, the smile as she gets off when we reach the room and she holds her palm out for the key. The light blinks green and she opens the door, holding it for me to push the cart through.

The room only has one king bed because I'm assuming that once she's done helping me wrap, she's going to call that guy and head his way.

She jumps on the bed and pats the spot in front of her. "Let's wrap."

I lean against the wall and stare at her for a moment, wanting desperately to know what she meant. I shouldn't get involved. I know that, but regardless I do.

"What did you mean you don't know what you're going to do?"

She tilts her head, not understanding, then she nods. "You mean about calling him?"

I nod and the room fills with tension.

She swallows hard and locks eyes with me. "I don't think I'm going to call him."

"Why?" I feel as if I'm on a tightrope, waiting for her answer.

"Because I'm not so sure the psychic had it right." She doesn't move, sitting on the bed with her legs crossed and her eyes on mine.

"Why?" I press.

She breaks eye contact and looks at her lap. "You really want me to say it?" She peeks up at me through her eyelashes.

Isn't that the resounding question? Do I? Because if I start this, she's not a one-night stand girl, not that I'd want that with her. I can't imagine that I'd be satisfied with just one time with this woman.

"Tre?" she says, her voice uncertain.

"Say it."

"Because in the last four days, he's no longer the one on my mind."

"Who is?" I need to hear her say my name. I don't know why. Fragile male ego? Maybe.

"Perhaps I should be turning these questions your way?" She leans back against the headboard.

I swallow hard. "What do you want to know?"

"Why did you kiss me? And if you say Callie, I'm calling bullshit."

I laugh, always impressed by Tessa's ability to cut right to it. Then I step forward toward the bed. "Simple. I wanted to. I apologize if I put you in an awkward situation."

She shakes her head and her teeth nibble at her bottom lip as I take another step toward her. My hands clench and release in preparation of touching her.

"Not at all."

"I worried that I overstepped."

She shakes her head again.

"What do you want, Tessa?"

She pulls her legs to her chest as if to protect herself from me. "You don't do relationships, and I don't do one-night stands."

"I think it might be different where you're concerned." The truth burns my tongue.

"I need more than *you think*."

"I know." It leaves my lips so fast, I'm unprepared, but it's the truth. I can't answer why after only four days with her, she's changed my way of thinking, but she has. That's all I know. "I want more with you. Is that what you want to hear? The last four days have been the most frustrating, most entertaining, most fun I've had in years and it's all because of you. But what do you want?"

184

"I'm scared," she says. "I've never felt this way before, especially so fast."

I stand at the edge of the bed and stare down at her. "I'm not going to cross the line unless you tell me you want me to. I'm scared too, but you're worth the risk."

"I have hang ups," she says abruptly.

"So do I. We'll work through them together, if that's what we decide."

She gets up on her knees. "I don't want you to leave me."

"Same here."

Our eyes meet with a powerful intensity, and all the what-if questions fade away. Time slows as she crawls toward me, the two of us acknowledging without words that something life-altering is about to happen.

The closer she moves to me, the more my nerves become hyper aware that this is about to happen. With our faces only millimeters apart, fear and excitement mix in my stomach. The uncertainty of what is about to happen is both thrilling and terrifying.

I tug her ponytail holder out, unleashing her dark hair to cascade down her shoulders. "Trust me, I'm in foreign territory too. Let's explore it together."

"Together," she says with a nervous tremble to her lips.

My heart pounds as the space between us becomes nonexistent and her eyes close, surrendering to the pull of the moment. I bend down, my lips finally meeting hers in a gentle, soft, questioning press. The kiss is a mere brush that sends shockwaves through my body.

We both pull away slightly, eyes locking, the palpable tension too great to deny. There are no more questions. We've opened the door and there's no going back the way we came.

She softly smiles and I match it, tugging on the dark strands of hair at the base of her neck, tilting her head and meeting her lips once more with the intensity of how badly I want her. I deepen the kiss, each movement of my lips filled with a hunger and urgency I've had for no other woman.

She locks her arms around my neck, her fingers running down the back of my head. My hands fall to her waist, pulling her flush against me, but she still doesn't feel close enough. The sensation overwhelms me, and I become lost in her.

Chapter Twenty-Two

TESSA

I've never felt like this with anyone else, which is both scary and exhilarating.

I'm pressed against his chest, his lips exploring my mouth, my hands wrapped around his neck. He closes our kiss, and I groan from the need to have his lips on mine still, but I can't complain because his lips travel along my jaw and down my neck. My head falls back, offering any inch of my body he demands.

"You're so beautiful," he says softly. His hands come to the hem of my T-shirt and the rough flesh of his calloused fingers grazes up my abdomen.

I inhale when one hand covers my breast, kneading it. I drag his mouth back on mine, and he swallows my moan, his hand pulling down the cup of my bra and his thumb running across my pebbled nipple. Our mouths turn frantic, messy, taking what the other offers.

Panting, we break apart, our hands exploring. He reaches back and takes the neck of his shirt, pulling it over his head and off his body. He tosses it on the nearby chair, and I giggle, my hands splaying out and touching every dip and valley of his muscles. There are tiny scars, raised skin, proof of the danger of his career choice.

"What's so funny?" he asks, reaching for the hem of my shirt and pulling it up off my body.

"That you still can't just toss your clothes wherever." I laugh again. "You had to make sure it hit the chair."

A rush of shivers runs up my spine when he frees me of my shirt and I'm kneeling on the mattress in just my bra with one cup down. He holds out my shirt, dangling it, and lets it go so it hits the carpet.

I shake my head. "That's only because it's *my* clothes."

"Not true." He gives me a chaste kiss, undoing my bra.

I reluctantly take my hands off his chest to free the bra from my arms and he drops it to the floor with a chuckle. His amusement only lasts a moment because our eyes meet, and all that lust spills over and our lips attach to one another as if they're magnets. His tongue slides into my mouth and we find the other's rhythm, perfecting something that I hope will be a part of my life for a long time to come.

I'm still scared and the small trembles hitting my body every couple of minutes show it, but I have to put trust in Tre. He's given me no reason not to. He could've left me so many times, but each opportunity he had, he stayed. That says something about his character.

"Tell me you have something," I ask, eager to have his weight over me.

"Yeah," he murmurs against my lips.

I pull my mouth off his delicious neck where the roughness of his five o'clock shadow has my imagination soaring with thoughts of his face between my legs. "Because you just brought them on this trip or because you didn't want to miss the opportunity if this happened between us?"

He slides his hand down the front of my pants, his finger dipping through my wet folds. "Sure."

I let loose a soft chuckle at his non-answer, but it doesn't matter. We can't deny what's happening between us, and it's not anything we could have predicted. "Because I'm irresistible."

His finger hooks inside me and my body jolts from the sensation. I grip his strong shoulders and my mouth hangs open with a low moan falling from my lips.

"You're so beautiful, Tessa. Especially right now. The way your skin is flushed the lightest shade of pink all over your body." He slides his hand out of my pants.

"Ugh, you're a tease."

"So impatient." He hooks his fingers in my jeans and tugs them down until I have to stand on the mattress to step out of them.

My core lines up to his face and he pulls me close to him, inhaling my scent and running his nose along my trimmed pussy. The act is indecent yet intoxicating, and I can't strip my eyes away from him. He licks me, focusing on my clit.

I grab his head and he nudges my legs wider.

"Damn it," I whimper because of course he's good at eating me out. Seems his tongue is an expert in everything sexual the same way his hands probably are at combat. My eyes flutter shut, and my fingers tighten on the short strands of hair on his head.

He runs his fingers through my wetness, teasing my opening and pushing two fingers inside me, hooking them to hit my G-spot while his tongue works my clit.

"It feels so good, don't stop," I say, thrusting my pussy into his face, unashamed.

He moans, his free hand moving across my lower back, holding me as still as he can make me.

"Yes." My voice grows louder. "Right there."

A warmth crawls through my body, my spine tingling, and the pressure builds and builds to an intensity that I can no longer contain. I come apart, and he slows his tongue until I don't see stars anymore.

Falling to my knees, I hurriedly grab at the button of his pants and tug them down, needing him inside me. "Where're the condoms?"

"In my bag. I'll get them."

He heads to his bag, stepping out of his jeans and dark boxer briefs, and oh my god. The man has the ass of a god.

When he returns, I snatch the condoms from his hand, tearing at the foil with my teeth. His eyes grow heated with a depth of fiery passion I've never seen. I use my finger and thumb to pull the condom out of the foil packet, and I place it on the tip of his huge dick, running it down his magnificent length. I should've known even this part of him would be perfect. My pussy tingles with the thought of having him fill me.

"Lie down," he says in a sweet yet demanding voice I know I could grow used to.

Doing as he says, I lie on my back.

"Spread your legs. I want to see your pussy." I open my legs, but they must not be open enough because he pushes them further, bringing my knees up to my ears. "So fucking perfect." Then he leans in and swipes his tongue from top to bottom, making me moan.

"Please, I need you." I reach down, ready to guide him in.

"Patience," he says, using his tip to tease my clit.

He takes my arms, locking his hands over my wrists, running his nose along my neck, whispering sweet things about my body and how much he's wanted me over the last few days. How I drove him insane, and he can't believe he's about to have me.

He's a master with his words, and he gets my body right where he wants it. Wet and needy. He slowly sinks into me, inch by thick inch, watching my face and not releasing my arms from above my head. My chest rises, my back arching off the mattress from the euphoric feeling settling inside me. My toes curl when he's in me to the hilt and doesn't move.

"Good?" he asks.

"Amazing."

He smiles and places his lips on mine, kissing me languidly and slowly. We have all night, and I'm already looking forward to the next time even though this one isn't over.

He circles his hips, his body moving over mine, then he releases my wrists, placing one hand on my cheek, staring into my eyes. Fuck, the intimacy is so thick I try not to allow my head to get involved.

His thrusts become harder and faster, and soon my legs wrap around his waist, and he's grinding into me. I love the hunger in his movements, the way I feel as if he wants me so badly he might go insane if he didn't have me. He doesn't want just any woman, but he wants me—my pussy, my tits, my writhing body under his.

I hold him, and sweat accumulates between our chests. My orgasm doesn't build this time, it comes on hard and fast and there's no holding it back until I feel as though I'm free falling, all the tension disappearing.

"Jesus, you're gorgeous when you come." He studies my face, but I'm still recovering from two of the best orgasms of my life. "Ride me?"

A grin is my only response.

He rolls us over, and I straddle his waist, taking his length in my hand and sinking down on him. He grabs my hips and guides the tempo as I ride him, my tits bouncing. The look in his eyes as he watches me on top of him, coupled with his dirty mouth, puts me on the brink of my third orgasm.

"These tits could make a smart man do some very stupid things." He moves his hands from my hips to my tits. I grab the headboard for more leverage and move my hips back and forth. "Oh fuck ..."

It's as though he's lost all ability to talk because he pants and growls until he pumps into me from below, stills, then holds my hips while he empties himself into the condom. He comes on my name, soft and sweet.

I collapse on him, and he wraps his arms around me, one hand running up and down my back. We catch our breaths until eventually, I roll over.

"I'll be right back." He kisses my cheek and heads into the bathroom. He returns, but before he does, I hear the shower turn on. "Shower?"

I grin at him. "I was thinking a nap and then round two?"

He chuckles and holds out his hand for me. I slide out of bed and accept his hand. Once we're in the warm shower, he wraps his arms around me from behind, kissing my neck.

"I want to ask you something," he says.

It's clear from the tone of his voice that whatever it is, it's serious. I want to complain that we're just coming off orgasms and this isn't the time to talk feelings. You can't always trust what comes out of your mouth.

"I want you to come home with me for Christmas," he says.

My eyes widen and I turn around, but he tightens his arms around my stomach and puts his head in the crook of my neck.

"Come on. Say yes."

"You're just saying this because I just gave you an orgasm."

"I'm asking you this because I want to spend the holidays with you." He sucks my earlobe into his hot mouth, twirling his tongue over it, and I suppress a shiver.

"That's a big step." There's obvious fear in my voice.

"Where did you think this would go? That you'd go home

on a plane tomorrow and I'd catch up with you after New Year's?"

"Actually." I turn around in his arms and he kisses my lips, his hands exploring my body. We've yet to even shampoo our hair or wash our bodies. "You said you're retiring?"

He smiles. "I am. Technically starting in January."

"Where are you going to live then?" I hate that we're having this conversation after just getting together, but I need details to ensure I'm not going to get my heart broken or have false expectations.

He shrugs. "I'm not sure. I can live anywhere."

I smile at him and place my hand on his cheek. "Then we have a lot of time. I'll just go home, and we'll get together after the holidays."

I'm selfishly relieved that I won't have to be separated from him for long chunks of time or worry about what might happen to him while he's deployed.

He rears back, removing his hands from my body. "I thought you said you were in this?"

"I am. I just don't think me bulldozing my way into your family holidays is the best first impression." I pick up the shampoo and he takes it, pouring some into his hand.

"But you were going to surprise douchebag at his family's house for Christmas?" He pushes his hands into my hair, working the shampoo through the strands.

"That was different, and I'm not sure that was ever a good idea. I might have temporarily lost my mind." Now that I've fallen for Tre, I can't even imagine trying to get Carter back. I mean, there's a reason we broke up. I never felt about him what I do for Tre. Not even remotely close.

"I really want you to come, and I know my mom would want you to come too. If you don't come to my parents', I'm staying here for the holidays with you."

"Tre," I sigh.

193

"What? Having me devour your pussy day and night doesn't sound like a great Christmas to you?"

I chuckle and swat him.

He's already days behind the time he was supposed to spend with his family. I'm not going to let any more time pass. "You're going home." I poke him in the chest, and he laughs. "And apparently, so am I. But you better warn them."

He pulls me into him. "They're going to love you."

I hope so because I've never felt so much pressure for a family to like me. "Yeah, nothing like Merry Christmas, I brought home a stray girl I met on a plane."

He chuckles, his hands urging my ass to wrap my legs around his waist. His dick is ready for round two and he rests my back on the shower wall. "Tell me you're happy."

I shake my head and stare into his eyes. "I honestly don't believe how happy I am right now."

His lips land on mine, and after he rushes back out to the bedroom to grab the condoms, he shows me how happy he is for the next twenty minutes until we have to shower all over again.

Chapter Twenty-Three

Tessa sits in the chair wearing my army T-shirt, wrapping the Christmas gifts. She's watching one of those Christmas movies on Lifetime or Hallmark, talking to herself about the characters.

I pull out my phone. I've been preparing to do this since the train when I knew I was going to make a move on her. I'm just thankful I didn't need to plead my case against some other guy. I would've hated that.

Me: Good news.

Lil'Bro: You ditched the girl and are finally coming home?

Me: Not exactly. But I am in Portland.

Mom: You're scaring me. What is it?

Lil'Sis: You guys are clueless, he's bringing the girl home.

Mom: What? Oh, there's a ton of stuff I need to get ready.

Me: Thanks B.

Lil'Sis: I knew it from the first text.

Lil'Bro: Who would have guessed that?

Lil'Sis: Get a clue and read between the lines.

Mom: So… we like this girl?

I glance at Tessa again. She's smiling like a loon at the television since the couple just got stuck under the mistletoe.

"Like their friends didn't plan that," she mumbles to herself.

Me: We really do.

Lil'Sis: You just made Mom tear up.

Lil'Bro: She'll probably be gone right after the holidays. This is Tre we're talking about.

Dad: Shut your mouth and have some respect.

Mom: When will you be home?

Me: Tomorrow morning. We'll catch a ride.

Mom: We can come get you.

Me: You have enough to do.

Lil'Sis: I'm so excited. Are you going to let them sleep in the same bed, Mom?

Lil'Bro: They shouldn't.

Dad: He's thirty-two years old. They can sleep where they want.

I wonder how Tessa will feel about that.

Mom: Love you. Be safe. See you tomorrow!

Me: See you all in the morning.

"Who are you texting? You should be over here helping me wrap." She crawls across the bed to me.

All I want to do is be inside her again. To hear the noises she makes because of what I'm doing to her body.

She straddles me and runs her hands down my chest. Her fingers run over the raised skin where I should have gotten stitches. "Do you have stories for all these little scars?"

"Yeah." My hands move to her hips. "But I'm not telling you any of them."

"I would like to officially apologize for being a complete brat that day on the plane. What you do for our country is amazing, and I was very unappreciative." She runs her hands along my biceps.

"I don't accept your apology. In fact, thank you for acting the way you did." She's only wearing her underwear under my shirt and the silk does nothing to hide the warmth of her pussy as she wiggles on my cock.

"Why would you thank me?"

"I'm not sure I would've paid you any attention. I loved the fact you called me GI Joe, your smart-mouth. It was like instant attraction for me."

Her head falls back in laughter. "That's the first I heard that. And you wouldn't have noticed me otherwise?" She tilts her head and raises her eyebrows.

"Oh, I'd already noticed you in security."

Her head falls to my chest. "I was a hot mess express at security."

I slide my hands up to her head and urge her to look up. "You were cute, and you did this thing where you blow a strand of hair off your forehead, and you had all of my attention. By the time you boarded the plane, I was already making excuses to talk to you after we arrived in Portland, but lucky me, Polly was eight months pregnant."

"So that's our meet-cute then?"

"I think so. The guy has to notice the woman first, don't you think?"

She presses her lips to mine, her breasts smashing against my chest from under the soft cotton of the T-shirt. I grab her ass and pull her closer, sliding my tongue into her mouth. We make out for a few minutes, but she's quick to tear her lips away.

"And when did you know it wasn't just physical?"

"When did you know you weren't calling douchebag anymore when you got here?"

She jabs her finger into my chest. "I asked you first."

"When I was convincing Judge Sullivan to get you out of jail, I agreed to play Santa. I wouldn't do that for just anyone." I run my hands up her back. "Now it's your turn."

"I think when you got me out of jail when you could've left me and continued on your way. It's the first time I thought I was doing the wrong thing by calling some other guy when I had an amazing guy right in front of me. But you constantly saying you didn't do relationships scared me."

I pull her closer, casting small kisses along her neck. "I'm sorry, I just never thought I would want a relationship at this point in my life. I have a lot of shit to figure out post-military service, but you're my game-changer. I've never had this pull to someone before and it keeps getting stronger and stronger. When I thought about letting you go find that guy, something inside me said I was making a huge mistake."

"You say all the right things." She grinds along my length.

"Do I?" My eyelids grow heavy with lust.

"Now you're going to get rewarded with an orgasm." She pushes me back a little bit and shimmies down my body, kissing her way down my chest, pulling the sheet away.

"You don't..."

She tugs the waistband of my boxer briefs down to rest under my balls. Wiggling on the bed to get comfortable, she grips the base with her right hand and stares up at me. As her mouth grows closer, her tongue slides out and licks around the tip.

My body reacts with a jolt, and she giggles. She knows exactly what to do. She twirls and licks at me, all the while she eye-fucks me. There's no way I can strip my gaze from her. My hand runs along her hair, making sure there's nothing obstructing the view of her mouth working my cock.

The more her tongue is on me, the more I lose the fight not to explode in her mouth. But when she twists her hand up and around, her mouth sinking down on my dick, the sound of her saliva, her moans, and my groans all mixed together in the room, I lose all willpower.

"I'm gonna come," I say, and she continues sucking my dick until my hips jolt up off the bed and I come in her mouth.

She waits until I'm completely done, swallows, and her eyes lock with mine her entire way back up my body.

"That was a great blow job for your first time," I say, and she laughs. We both know it's not her first time, but I'm going to pretend it was.

"I read a lot of books."

We both laugh and I roll her over, kissing her neck, my hands running up under my shirt, molding to her tits.

"As much as I love seeing you in my T-shirt, I'd like it back now." I strip it off her body with her help, and my mouth descends on her nipple, sucking and licking until it's a tight bud.

Soon another condom is out of the box and I'm deep inside her. I'm not sure I'll ever have enough of her.

After a shower, we opted for a nap, and when we woke, Tessa insisted that we finish wrapping the gifts while watching *Christmas Vacation*. She schooled me on my wrapping job, and I was demoted to the tape guy in the end.

The next morning, she comes out of the bathroom, and I actually draw back for a second. Her hair is blown dry, curled, and her makeup done to perfection. She's absolutely gorgeous, not that she isn't gorgeous without the makeup. Hell, I fell for her without makeup.

"What?" She looks at me, sitting in the chair to put on her socks, covering up her cute pink polished toes.

"You look amazing."

"Oh, you mean you don't prefer my not exhausted, rundown road trip look with a pony on top of my head, face bare, and overall girl next door look best?"

I hold out my arms, and she walks over and stands between my legs. I take her hands in mine, our fingers playing with one another's. "I prefer the pony and no makeup look, but I'll take this one."

She shakes her head with a smile. "Bullshit."

I raise my hand. "I swear."

"Well, I like this whole jeans and a sweater thing you've got going on. The cologne is making me all hot and wet." She puts her knees on either side of my waist and settles over my lap. "How much time do we have?"

"We could stay here all day if you want," I say, not upset at all if she chose that.

"You're not getting out of seeing your family, Abner."

I raise both eyebrows.

"I was just trying it out. But Tre fits much better."

I smack her ass cheeks with my hands, and she yelps. "Good. Otherwise, I was going to give you a name you wouldn't like."

She slides off me, and I miss her immediately. She puts on her short ankle boots, her coat, and we pack up the luggage cart I went and grabbed earlier this morning. I pull up the Uber app, and after we get downstairs, we climb into the car ready to take us to my hometown, Climax Cove.

Once we're on the road, she straightens in her seat. "I don't have anything. I can't show up empty-handed."

"You're not. You're bringing their most favorite person." I waggle my eyebrows, which has her rolling her eyes.

"I need a bottle of wine or something." She digs into her purse and pulls out her uncle's wallet.

She's looking through it and I'm watching her, wondering what her game plan is here. My parents won't care if she brings anything.

"Oh my," she says, digging into a small cut in the leather.

"What is it?" I look closer.

She pulls out a picture of a little girl who's maybe five or so and a man and a woman. They're at an ice skating rink, each parent holding one of her hands. When she turns it over, it reads, "Five years old. Merry Christmas, Uncle Al."

"That's you and your parents?" I ask, and she nods. "You were cute."

She looks up at me with tears in her eyes. "Why did he have this? I always felt like such a nuisance, as if my parents dying ruined his life."

"He probably didn't want to lose it. You can tell he looked at it often." I point out the frayed edges.

Her shoulders fall. "There's something else in here." She squeezes her fingers and twists the leather wallet to get it out. "What the hell?"

She pulls out five one-hundred-dollar bills.

"But he didn't have any money."

"He obviously kept it in there for emergencies." I smile at her, hoping it gives her some peace that her uncle did care about her and probably missed her parents as well.

"Here." She holds out the five hundred dollars.

I hold up my hands. "I'm not taking that."

"Yes, you are. I owe you even more." She drops the bills in my lap.

I catch the driver's eyes on me in the rearview mirror. God knows what he's thinking right now.

I feel her anxiety about coming home with me, and I can't argue that I don't feel a little of the same. I've never brought someone home before. I pick up the hundred-dollar bills and put them in her purse. "It is your uncle's money. You keep it and spend it. Me and you are square."

I eye her hard and she nods, but I have a feeling I'm going to have to constantly check that she didn't sneak it into one of my bags.

"Now come here. You're way too far away." I hold out my arm and she smiles, snuggling into me.

As we drive, her hand that was on my chest drops and her steady breathing blows into my neck. I smile, staring out the window as we grow closer to my parents' house. I can't wait to introduce her and find out if they love her as much as me. If they'll see how great we are together, how even though we're opposite in so many ways, we just fit.

When the car pulls up to my childhood home, I spot the huge ass sign welcoming me home and shake my head. I nudge Tessa and she stretches, but I dodge her hand right before she hits me.

"We're here," I whisper.

She bolts up, and her eyes widen. "I need to freshen up. Why didn't you tell me?" She looks out the window, spots the sign, and turns back to me. "How cute. I love your mom already."

We're not out of the car ten seconds before my family barrels out the door as if they were watching out the window.

"Tre!" My mom attaches herself to me immediately.

Dad says hi to Tessa first, and they shake hands as she introduces herself. Brynn slides in to hug me before Dad, and Mom rushes over to Tessa, pulling her into a hug. Tessa looks at me over my mom's shoulder and it's clear she's not used to so much affection. Although she's allowed me to touch her anywhere and everywhere, I've noticed she can be skittish with others. But she pats my mom's back, so baby steps.

"We're so happy to have you, Tessa. Merry Christmas," my mom says.

"Thanks for having me."

"Where's the pain in my ass? He needs to help me with the bags and all the presents," I say about my brother.

"He's probably going to the bathroom and leaving the toilet seat up," Brynn complains before saying hello to Tessa but reading her body language that she's not a hugger.

"It was one time. Give me a fucking break." My brother saunters outside wearing his pajama pants and a T-shirt.

"Language!" Mom scolds. "How nice of you to get dressed. We have a guest now."

I'm laughing at my family, missing all these moments. I'd forgotten how much I love being here. They love me for me.

It takes me too long to notice what it seems the rest of my family has. Tessa is standing still, her mouth hanging open as she stares at my brother in disbelief.

"Tessa?" he says. "What are you doing here?"

She glances at me and back at my brother. "Carter?"

"The douchebag?" I clarify, but no one has to tell me because it's clear in both of their faces.

Tessa was traveling across country to reunite with my little brother.

Chapter Twenty-Four

I've never heard that tone of voice from Tre. Disregarding Carter, I turn back to Tre, but he's already at my back, his hand on my hip.

"I had no idea," I say.

"What are we missing?" Brynn asks, smirking as if she binge-watches old soap operas in her spare time and this is her chance to see one in person.

"Um..." I shift in place.

"Dad, do you mind taking our stuff in? I have to talk to Tessa." Tre's hand slides into mine.

He walks me into his house, up the stairs, and into a room, shutting the door behind us. My heart pounds rapidly. I want to look out the window or pinch myself because there's no way this is real. Carter is Tre's brother? What the hell, fate? Is this some fuck you from karma for not putting a wreath on my uncle's gravesite?

"Explain," Tre says, his back against the door, his arms crossed.

Where is my Tre? This version of him is something new and I suspect might be more in line with Army Tre.

"Carter and I went on some dates, and I broke it off because I didn't really feel anything. But then I went to that psychic, and she made it sound like he was the one."

I look around the room and realize this must be his child-hood bedroom. I'm not sure his mom has touched it since he left. There are football trophies lined up along a top shelf, his letterman jacket hung on a hook by the closet. A dark blue comforter covers a queen-size bed, and there are a few pictures of what must have been his closest friends in high school. It's just a regular high school kid's bedroom.

"What exactly did the psychic say?" he asks.

I sit on the edge of the bed before I pass out. "Why does it matter? You don't even believe in it. You were making fun of me."

He blows out a breath. This isn't exactly ideal for me either, and now I'm in their family home admitting that I got a plane four days ago to try to convince their one son I was the woman for him, and now I've fallen for the other. What if Polly hadn't been on the plane? What if we would've landed safely in Portland? I shake my head because now that I've been with Tre, it's clear fate intervened and I'm supposed to be with him.

I look up from my twisted fingers in my lap at him.

"Did you sleep with him?" His voice and his facial expres-sion are both firm.

"No!" I screech. "Is that what you're so upset about? I'm sorry. I'm just as surprised as you."

He pushes off the door with a sigh and sits next to me on the bed, grabbing my hand and putting it in his lap. "I'm sorry for being angry. I'm just shocked and I..."

He doesn't have to say it, but I think he feels a little insecure.

"Me too." I turn toward him, taking his other hand. "But please know that you are the one I want. I'm so happy that I met you on this trip and we fell into what we have now. I'm not sure why I ever thought Carter was the one for me. I have no feelings for him."

He nods, but I can see he's still not completely sold. Hopefully in time he'll realize the truth of my words.

Tre slides one hand out from holding mine, and his knuckles graze down my face as he stares into my eyes. "I feel the same way."

"You don't love Carter either?" I joke at the worst time ever, but I do get rewarded with a small smile.

We lean toward one another, and our lips meet. Our chemistry hasn't been affected by this new revelation because after only a few seconds of our tongues tangling, he's urging me up and over to straddle him. If only I could be with him right now, convince him with my body that he's mine and I don't want anyone else. Maybe me coming for Carter and what happened between us was what was supposed to happen. Maybe the psychic was talking about *Tre*.

"God." He breaks away, panting for breath. "I wish we were back at the hotel."

I bet what he really wishes is that he never would've brought me home.

"Me too." My hands cling to him, and I run my core against his length, desperate to get as close to him as I can before he pulls away.

His hands land on my hips, but he stops me from grinding. "Okay, we have to go downstairs and talk to everyone. I think everyone is confused."

I get up off of him and straighten my shirt and pants, turning to look in the full-length mirror by his door to check my lipstick after our small makeout session. "I'm so embarrassed to go down there."

He takes my hand and opens the door.

"I didn't do anything!" I hear Carter say from downstairs.

We walk down, and the voices lower in volume when they hear us coming. They're all in the family room where a giant tree is sprinkled with lights and what looks like homemade ornaments. They're the kind I can tell Tre, Carter, and Brynn made as they were growing up. The television is on some morning show, and a wood fire burns in the fireplace. The mantel above the fireplace is adorned with family photos over the years. Stockings with each family member's name stitched into them hang across the mantel, and my heart squeezes when I see them. It's the ultimate sign of belonging, of family.

His mom is on the chaise lounge while his dad paces in front of the fireplace. Carter is in a chair by the window and Brynn is stretched out with her feet on the ottoman. They all straighten when we stop in the archway of the room.

This is a family. A true family, and I just ruined their Christmas.

Tre opens his mouth, but I step forward first. He shouldn't have to do this. "First of all, it's nice to meet you all and thank you for having me in your home. So... this is going to sound weird, and I promise you I'm not crazy." I look at Carter. "I had no idea Tre was your brother." I turn to Tre, and he nods. "Four days ago, I boarded a plane to Portland to come find you, Carter."

Brynn chuckles. "Someone up there must love you to intervene."

Tre's mom swats her leg.

"It wasn't because I was in love with you or anything," I say to Carter.

"Gee, thanks," he says, rolling his eyes.

"You didn't have strong feelings for me either. We went on a handful of dates."

Tre blows out a breath while Carter looks chagrined because he knows there was no love connection between us.

"Then why were you coming here?" Brynn asks.

Tre's mom shoots her a warning glare to shut up, but Brynn shrugs. And she has the right to ask the question. It's the obvious one I'm sure they're all thinking.

I look over my shoulder at Tre and back at the family. "A psychic told me to."

Brynn's feet hit the floor and she sits up, probably thinking I'm a crazy nut and she needs to protect her family. In the meantime, his dad stops pacing and looks at Tre in confusion. Carter stares blankly while his mom softly smiles at me as though she pities me.

I suck in a deep breath. "I was skeptical too, but she saw I had just lost my bakery." I close my eyes when I say it. Talk about them thinking Tre brought home a loser.

"You're a baker?" his mom asks.

"She's really good too," Carter chimes in. "She makes these sugar cookies that I swear challenge..." He stops when he realizes he might insult his mom.

Did Tre just growl behind me?

"I had to close my bakery, and the psychic saw how that was my first love, so I started to believe her when she told me other things. I was in the right headspace to listen to her, I suppose... I'd just buried my great-uncle and he'd raised me since my parents died when I was nine."

His mom's face falls, Brynn covers her mouth with her hand, and his dad places a hand on my shoulder, giving me his condolences. I'm really knocking this out of the park.

"I'm okay, honestly. Anyway... she told me things that I assumed meant she was talking about you." I point at Carter. "But now that I think about it, it might've been about either of you."

"What did she say?" Brynn asks, leaning forward a bit.

"Brynn, stop it," their mom says.

I turn to Brynn. "Just that he had dark hair, he helps people, to head west, and that we both had faults, but if we worked through them together, I'd have everything I ever dreamed of." I leave out all the family stuff the psychic said because I do not want these people to think they're supposed to welcome me with open arms. Especially now.

"Carter doesn't help people," Brynn says, forehead wrinkled.

"I'm in IT, dumbass. I help people every day," Carter says.

Tre's mom stands, putting up her hands. "Okay, everyone, can we behave? We have a guest. Continue, Tessa." She motions to me and sits back down.

"Then my seatmate went into labor on the plane and Tre delivered the baby."

His mom smiles at Tre, clearly proud of him.

"And we ended up having to share the last rental car, and for the last four days, we've been working together to make it here. During that time, I fell hard for Tre. And when we got to Portland, I decided not to call you, Carter, because I knew my feelings for Tre were so much more than I ever felt for you."

"Thanks again for that."

Carter's dad shoots him a warning glare.

"Then Tre asked me to come home with him. Never in a million years did I think you were brothers."

"Of course you didn't." His dad smiles at me and goes behind me to Tre. "Then this is settled. Let's have brunch. Your mom's been cooking all morning."

"I'm starving." Brynn stands and follows her dad into the kitchen.

His mom comes over to me and runs her hand down my arm. "Welcome to our home."

"Thank you." I relax a bit at how they've all reacted, but there's still some lingering anxiety that Tre may not be able to brush this off as easily as the rest of his family.

I'm about to follow them into the kitchen when Carter steps toward me. "Can I talk to you for a second?"

Another disgruntled sound comes out of Tre, and he rolls his eyes, but he kisses my temple and walks into the kitchen.

I turn to Carter. "What's up?"

"I... I don't know. I just felt like we should talk, but I'm not sure what to say."

"This is awkward, but I'm sure with time, it will become normal." At least I hope so.

"So, you and my brother, huh?"

I nod, biting my bottom lip.

"Well, I'm happy for you both."

I give him a relieved smile. "Thanks, Carter."

He steps in and hugs me, taking me by surprise. I'm uncomfortable, but this is his way of calling a truce, so I hug him back.

"He's not easy," he whispers. "But he's worth it."

"Oh, I know. We're not exactly alike, but I think that's what draws us together."

"Probably."

A throat clears and we step away from one another.

"The food is getting cold." Tre's arms are crossed and resting on his chest, his eyes boring a hole right into Carter.

If Carter notices, he doesn't seem to care. He squeezes my hand and slides by his brother into the kitchen.

"You okay?" I ask Tre.

He crosses the room, takes me into a hug, and kisses me until I'm panting for breath.

"Jeez, get a room, you two," Brynn says with a plate full of food in her hand. "FYI, we started the Christmas movie list without you." She sits on the couch and grabs the remote.

Tre doesn't respond, leading me into the kitchen. But unlike before, the warmth of his hand doesn't make me feel as though everything will be okay. If I didn't know better, I'd think Tre is struggling with this the most.

Chapter Twenty-Five

The entire day, everyone appears to be okay with this new surprise predicament.

I'm still in shock that she was on her way to win my brother's heart. As hard as I'm trying to push it out of my mind, I can't help but think back to the last time I was stuck in this situation.

Mom decides to push off sugar cookie day until tomorrow because she wants us to show Tessa around Climax Cove. I'd rather stay in the house, but Mom's waited all this time for me to get home.

"Will you please move your leg away from mine?" Brynn says to Carter in the back of my parents' SUV. The two of them are shoved in the third seat at the very back.

"I'm a tall guy, okay?"

"Well, you don't need to man spread."

"What can I say? I need the room."

I shake my head at Carter. I hold Tessa's hand in the middle row while my dad drives, and my mom keeps pointing out everything and explaining what it is to Tessa. She's acting interested, but I can tell her mind is somewhere else. Probably wondering why I can't seem to get back to who I was only a few hours ago. And I want to. I really do.

Dad parks downtown along the curb near the little Santa's village by the marina. No doubt the maze to reach Santa and get a picture with him will be alive and kicking.

"I'm not doing the maze," Brynn says, climbing out of the third row, groaning the entire time as though she's ninety.

"Tessa, do you want to do the maze?" my mom asks.

We all stare at the makeshift maze the town puts together, leading the little ones to Santa.

"Sure," Tessa says, but I take her hand and pull her in the opposite direction.

"She really means no," I say.

"You guys are no fun. I need grandchildren," Mom whines. "But not yet. Live your lives."

We laugh because that's her usual saying. She wants grandkids, but she's not ready for any one of us to have them yet. I'm not sure if she'd mind if it were me since I'm the oldest, but she'd never put that pressure on me.

"Double D's?" Tessa asks as we head down the sidewalk and she spots the sign.

"The town diner," I explain.

"All the names are so cute." She looks around at more of the local businesses. "Nail Me Hardware?" She chuckles.

"Yeah, not sure he thought that one out when he named it."

We walk into a few shops, and I'm happy to see Tessa spend some of that five hundred dollars on a mug. My mom and sister secretly buy a few things Tessa says she likes at the soap place, and we end up at the Happy Daze Bar & Grill for lunch.

Dane, the owner—who happens to be the father of my best friend in high school, Toby—is behind the bar. He inherited the business from family and even has another location in a nearby town now.

"That's not Tre, is it?" Dane puts his hand over his eyes as if the lights are making him see things.

"Hey, Mr. Murray," I say with a smile.

He comes around the bar to stand in front of me. "Oh please, you're old enough to call me Dane now." I shake his hand, but he pulls me into a hug. "Thanks for your service," he whispers before releasing me. He eyes Tessa at my side. "And who's this?"

I place my hand on the small of her back. "This is Tessa, my..." I realize that we haven't really classified one another.

"Girlfriend! Seriously." Brynn shakes her head and rolls her eyes.

I clarify by looking at Tessa for reassurance, and she smiles at me.

"Girlfriend it is," I say.

Dane laughs, full-on belly laughing. He slowly stops and sets his attention on Tessa. "You have to be patient with guys like us." He waves his finger between him and me. "Once we fall, we tend to not know which way is up and end up fucking up a lot."

"You're putting me in your category?" I ask, joking. "Dane's wife runs Mad Hatter across the street," I inform Tessa. "She's a baker too."

"You're a baker?" he asks Tessa, eyebrows raised.

Her head tilts right and left as if she's not sure.

"She is. She just needs to find the right place to showcase her skills." I put my arm around Tessa's shoulders.

"Blah," Brynn says and puts her finger in her throat. "I need to eat before I lose my appetite with all this lovey-dovey stuff." She winks then heads over to the table my parents and brother are at.

"Where are you from?" Dane asks Tessa, looking across the street and back.

"New York City."

"Oh man, I had an idea, but that's not going to pan out with you living across the country. You live there now too?" Dane asks me, going back around the bar and grabbing the white slip of paper at the top of the register. He glances at it quickly.

"No. I just retired, and all my stuff is back in Georgia. I came home for the holidays but have to go back."

"Then how did you two meet?" He grabs a couple of glasses and makes the drinks I assume were on the slip he pulled from the register.

We both look at one another. "On a plane," we say in unison.

"It's a long story," I say, not wanting to get into it. Especially the part where she was on her way here for my brother. "How's Toby?" Just saying his name makes my chest prick.

"He's good. Living in Portland. Single." He huffs. "I thought for sure he'd settle down by now."

I nod, not adding much. We both can assume who Dane thinks Toby would have settled down with had the big blowup not happened.

"Well, we're gonna go." I thumb toward the table where my parents are.

"Yeah, I'll stop by when things slow down."

I fist bump him and we walk over to my parents' table. My mom looks at me, trying to decipher if I'm okay. I love my mom, but I really wish she wasn't always so suffocating with wanting to talk about my feelings.

I push back all the bullshit from this morning. All the bullshit from my past.

I'm back home and that's what matters. Plus, I have Tessa right next to me and this is everything I didn't know I wanted.

I can't be choosy over the way I got it. Sometimes things are messy before they work out.

* * *

After a marathon of three Christmas movies, I had to wake Tessa to get her upstairs. Brynn and Carter stayed up for another one, and my parents were already asleep.

Now, the morning light shines through my curtains, and I stare at Tessa sleeping next to me. She's wearing one of my T-shirts, but it's tangled and has risen up to just under her tits—during her sleep or with the help of my hand, I'm not sure which.

Needing to get rid of this anxiety building inside me, I slowly get out of bed and tiptoe over to my duffle bag. I change into my running gear and quietly leave my parents' house.

Turning on my music after my earbuds are in, I stretch. I haven't run since the day before I got on the plane. I start with a light jog around my parents' neighborhood, if you can call it that. The houses are far apart with a lot of land between, but there's only one road in and out. Thankfully, they haven't gotten hammered with a ton of snow, so I'm able to move from my jog to a good pace once I've warmed up.

It isn't until I get to the park that I see someone familiar running toward me. She smiles and waves, and I slow my pace until I'm walking.

"Oh my god, Tre?" Theresa doesn't break her stride, throwing herself into me, giving me no choice but to hug her.

"Hey, how are you? Home for the holidays?" I ask, pulling off my hat, letting the air cool me down.

"Yeah. Got in the end of last week."

We stand there, clearly uncomfortable with this impromptu meetup.

I haven't seen Theresa since senior year. On every other visit home, I've somehow managed to avoid her. Theresa, Toby, and I were the "Triple Ts" and hung out together all the time. Until it all got fucked up.

"Oh hey, I heard you brought a girl home?" She smiles. "I heard she's really pretty."

As usual, it doesn't take long for word to spread around our small town.

"Tessa, yeah." I nod.

"That's great. I'm glad you found your someone."

I glance at her glove-covered hand and wonder if there's a ring. Mom usually tells me everything, but she might've kept that bit of information to herself.

Theresa must notice me looking and takes off her glove. "Not yet. Still searching."

"Well, you'll find someone."

"I'm not really in a rush. I like my life in Seattle."

I can't believe how uncomfortable this is. There was a time Theresa knew all my deepest secrets. She was the person I would've talked to about my feelings for Tessa and how she dated Carter before me. But Theresa ruined that for us. She ruined the Triple Ts.

"I guess I better get going. Merry Christmas, Tre." She hugs me again, then takes a moment and stares at me before she smiles and runs by me.

"Merry Christmas," I mumble and put my hat back on.

I run again, my mind filling with thoughts of what happened all those years ago. I was so young and naive, and Theresa manipulated the situation.

By the time I get back to my parents' house, my head is another layer of fucked up. Seeing Theresa pried open a box I've kept shut for over a decade, but now it feels almost as raw as it was the day it all went down.

I open the back door of my parents' house, thinking I'll be

sneaking in because it's so early. I figure I'll prepare a coffee for Tessa and bring it up to her, then take a shower.

The laughter I hear when I step in to take off my shoes nauseates me. I walk into the kitchen, and sure enough, Carter and Tessa are at the table, drinking coffee.

Carter looks at me and smiles. "Still with the dedication of an Army Ranger." I ignore his razz to grab a water. "I'm going to go shower."

Carter leaves the room and Tessa comes up behind me, wrapping her arms around my waist and pressing her head to my back.

"You were gone this morning when I woke up." She places a kiss on my back, and I circle around and kiss her lips briefly.

"I'm sorry. I wanted to get a run in before today got crazy."

She places her hands on either side of my face and stares into my eyes. "Are you okay? Are we okay?"

I should just tell her that I'm struggling with this, worried about losing her. That I can't handle the fact she dated my brother. What if she wakes up one day and decides she doesn't like how grumpy I am, or how neat I prefer things? How I tend to stick to myself rather than be the life of the party? But I swallow all of my fears. It's way too early in our relationship to go piling all my baggage at her feet.

"We're perfect." I kiss her again, keeping my lips on hers longer this time.

But when I pull away, concern is still etched in her face. She doesn't believe me, and why should she? I'm lying.

What a great start to our relationship.

Chapter Twenty-Six

TESSA

I'm in the kitchen with Tre's mom, Gwen, helping to prepare the sugar cookie dough while the guys are in the family room watching football. Brynn went out to meet up with some of her friends.

"So, what's your secret?" Gwen asks, breaking eggs on the counter and putting them in the bowl.

"I don't really have a secret. My leavening is equal parts baking powder and baking soda. I don't like my cookies too thick. But it's not like I have some ingredient that no one's heard of. Plus, let's remember my bakery closed, so my cookies couldn't have been that good."

She stares at me a moment, then turns around and digs into her cabinet. I continue to level the dry ingredients for her according to her recipe.

She returns and puts a bowl in front of me. "You make yours, and I'll make ours."

"No." I shake my head. "I am not doing a competition."

She laughs. "There's enough love in this house for two sugar cookie recipes. Plus, Tre might strangle Carter if he hears about your sugar cookies from him one more time."

I chuckle, but she's right. It's like Carter's throwing it in Tre's face because he earns a scowl each time he talks about tasting my sugar cookie.

"Most of all, I want to taste them," she says.

"Are you sure?"

Her hand touches mine. "Very."

I nod, and since she was going to do a double batch, I assemble her other room-temperature ingredients, and she says she'll do one batch.

We can hear the boys arguing and screaming in the other room. Carter and Tre really go after one another in regard to the players and teams and who is better.

"Are they always like that?" I ask.

She laughs. "Yes. So competitive with one another. Carter mostly. I think it's hard when your older brother is Tre Russell. He was the prom king, captain of the football team, has a Silver Star from the military. I've always tried to tell them that they each have their own special qualities, but they're pretty different for brothers."

We work side by side in silence since I'm not sure what to add to what she's said. I've dated both her boys, so I know how different they are.

"And then we have Brynn, who can't keep her smart-mouth shut. But growing up with two brothers keeps you on your toes, so I can't really blame her." Gwen chuckles and starts her mixer. "Do you have any siblings?"

"No. It's just me." I hand mix my dough, which I haven't done since I was perfecting my recipe a long time ago.

"That's hard." I hear the motherly concern in her voice.

"Please, all Cooper Rice is is a pretty face." Carter comes in and heads to the fridge, grabbing some beers.

"Cooper Rice is the best quarterback the league has seen in five years." Tre joins us in the kitchen but goes to the cupboard.

"Why do we argue about these players who make millions to play?" Abe follows his sons into the room and hovers over Gwen's shoulder. She pinches some dough, and he opens his mouth. Then he looks at my bowl. "What's this? Two kinds of sugar cookies?"

"She insisted," I say.

Gwen laughs. "I did. It's only fair. Plus, I wanted to see what all the hype was about."

"The hype is only coming from Carter," I say without thinking.

Tension fills the room once more. Why did I say anything? Damn it. I just didn't want them to expect too much. They'll taste my cookies and find them blah, like all of New York City.

The boys head back into the family room without saying anything else. Tre's been so distant. Even in bed last night, he barely touched me. And since I laid awake most of the night, I know.

We wrap our dough in Saran Wrap and put them in the fridge.

"Can we talk?" Gwen asks. "Maybe go for a walk?"

I nod. "Sure."

We go to the back door and put on our coats, hats, gloves, and boots. She leashes their dog Jazzy, and we leave without telling the guys. I'm a little nervous about why Gwen wants to talk to me alone, but I try not to show it.

I'm impressed when Jazzy doesn't pull on the leash. She just walks beside Gwen.

We both don't say a word for the first minute or two of our walk and then Gwen breaks the silence. "He'll get there. Just give him time."

I glance at her and nod. "Okay."

"Listen, Tessa, I know we just met, and I don't know a lot about you. I also know I'm not *your* mom, but I am *a* mother. If I had passed when my kids were younger, I would hope that another mom would step in at some point to offer my kids advice. Advice one can only gain by living it."

I don't say anything, because my throat clogs with emotion that's going to be released in a rush of tears if I open my mouth.

"This situation isn't ideal. I know you and Tre are new, and I see the way he looks at you, but even if you two don't work out, please..." She stops and grabs my hand. "You can come to me. I would want someone to do that for my kids, and I'm sure your mom would want the same for you. You probably think I'm crazy, but you'll understand when you're a mother someday."

"He's different," I admit.

She inhales deeply. "That's my Tre. But he really likes you. I think he might even love you, but I'd never tell him that. He's not ready to hear it."

Her words make the air rush from my lungs. "Why?"

She smiles. "You scare him. Whatever he feels for you scares him."

"But why? I mean, I'm scared too, but I'm scared to lose him. That he'll wake up one day and realize I'm a failure."

"Don't you dare," she says with a stern tone. She unhooks Jazzy when we reach an open field. "Don't you call yourself a failure. So, you opened a bakery and for some reason it wasn't successful? I know it took a damn bit of courage to open that bakery in the first place."

I nod, a tear slipping and falling down my cheek.

"That doesn't make you a failure. You're a winner just for trying. It's a heck of a lot more than a lot of people ever do. It just means you have to get up and try again. Which sucks, it does, but you keep getting up when life knocks you down. You stand with dignity and try again."

Her words make me feel a little better. "Thanks."

She puts her arm around me. So much of her feels like Tre. He must take after her the most.

"Did Tre tell you why he joined the military?" she asks.

I think for a moment. "I thought he just decided that's what he wanted to do."

She looks down the street. "No. He was supposed to go to college. He had two best friends growing up. Toby, who is Dane's son, the guy you met at the bar? And Theresa, who lives down that way." She points down the road.

"Okay…"

"He'd probably kill me for saying this, for telling you since he hasn't, but Toby and Theresa dated, and in the end, it broke them all apart. By senior year, Tre rarely talked to either one of them. Around midyear, he was all set to attend Oregon on a football scholarship. Around here, there isn't a lot of that, so it was a big deal. The whole town was super proud of him."

"He didn't tell me any of that," I say, hurt that he didn't trust me with the information. Maybe we just haven't gotten to the point where we'd talk about it, but I suspect he purposely hasn't brought it up.

We walk farther along a trail, and Jazzy comes back with a stick in her mouth.

"He never talks about it. Acts as if it didn't happen. But this is what changed it all… Theresa snuck into his bedroom one night and confessed she loved him. She tried to kiss him, and he denied her, telling her he was going to tell Toby." Gwen shakes her head. "What was she thinking?"

My stomach sinks.

"The next day, he went over to tell Toby, but Theresa was already there and told Toby that Tre had hit on her, tried to kiss her. They ended up fighting, and it just…" She shakes her head again and frowns. "It changed him. He decided to skip out on the scholarship and join the military. Left right after graduation."

"I'm so sorry," I say. My chest squeezes, thinking of how hurt Tre must've been back then and how this thing with his brother must be extra hard for him.

"Kids are so stupid. But that Theresa—" She cuts off her words, almost as if she were going to say something mean and stopped herself.

It all makes so much more sense now. His reaction to me dating his brother, his mention of all the Dear John letters his military buddies received...

"So, finding out that Carter was the guy you were coming here for probably brings that all up again."

"You don't think he thinks he was just a convenience. And now that we're here, I really want Carter, do you?"

She shrugs. "I have no idea. But I felt you should know what you're working against."

"Thank you." This thing with his brother is going to be harder for Tre to get over than I'd assumed.

"You're welcome. I think he's found something special with you, and I don't want him to blow it." She clips the leash back on Jazzy. "Ready to warm up?"

"Yes," I say, rubbing my hands together. It's not super cold, but I'm ready to go back in.

We head into the house while my head swims with things I can do to reassure Tre. When we're inside, we take off our boots and coats. All I want to do is go over to Tre and crawl in his lap, but I stop when I hear the shouting.

Carter and Tre are screaming at each other.

Gwen touches my arm and walks by me into the family room. "What's going on? May I remind you both, you're brothers and family comes before all else."

I'm already emotional, so tears well in my eyes instantly.

It doesn't take me long to know what I have to do. I sneak upstairs, pack my bags, and write a note to Tre. I won't ruin someone else's family. Especially one this nice. I know what it's like not to have one, and I can't do that to these lovely people.

I tiptoe down the stairs, listening to them continuing to argue.

"When you have someone in your life, get back to me," Tre says.

"I had her. She didn't want me," Carter says in return.

It's clear they're arguing about me, so I slide into my boots, grab my coat, and quietly shut the back door behind me. I take one last look at the house, wipe my tears, and walk away.

I never imagined leaving would be this hard after such a short time. But this is what's best.

Chapter Twenty-Seven

TRE

I cannot believe Carter is coming at me with this bullshit right now.

"You're going to fuck this up for yourself." Carter gives me a disgusted look.

"What are you talking about?" I scowl at him.

He points toward the kitchen. "Mom and Tessa are gone, and so is Jazzy. Probably because of the way you acted when we were in there getting more snacks and drinks. You didn't even acknowledge her. What's wrong with you?"

I sip my drink and stare at the television. "Nothing."

"Then get your head out of your ass. When she gets back, show her how much she means to you."

I roll my eyes. He has no idea what he's talking about. The guy's never been in a serious relationship in his life.

"You need to get over yourself. Have you seen the way she looks at you?"

Dad sits in his chair, watching the game as if he doesn't hear us. He's always been one to stay out of our fights, thinking we should iron it out ourselves.

"Or hell the way you look at her," Carter adds. "You love her."

I scoff. "I barely know her."

Carter stands and raises his arms. "Dad, talk some sense into him. He's about to blow his entire opportunity with Tessa because of some shit that went down over a decade ago."

My dad doesn't say anything.

I stand. "This has nothing to do with that."

"Yes, it does. I get it. They were your best friends, and you were the innocent party."

I point at him. "You don't know shit. It cut me. How do you trust anyone if you can't trust your best friend? I saw her this morning, and she acted like nothing fucking happened. As if I didn't change my entire life path because of what she did."

"And you should have told her to go fuck herself."

"I don't work that way. I don't see you bringing anyone home, so why are you lecturing me?" I sit back down on the edge of the couch. "When you have someone in your life, get back to me." Rage veils my vision so that I can't even concentrate on the game.

"I had her. She didn't want me," he says.

I'm back on my feet, over him, his shirt fisted in my hand.

"Whoa!" Dad comes over, putting his hand on my chest. "That's enough."

Mom barrels into the room. "What's going on? May I remind you both that you're brothers and family comes before all else."

I drop Carter, and he falls into the couch cushion. Mom continues to lecture us, then she and Dad argue.

"Talk some sense into him, Mom. He's going to lose her," Carter continues.

"It's none of his business," I say, done with him.

"She's way too good for you," Carter says, and it takes everything inside me not to punch him right in the face.

"Fuck this."

I stomp off to the basement, strip off my sweatshirt, put on the gloves, and hit the punching bag dad installed when I was in high school. It was his way of getting Carter and me to stop fighting. He said take it out on the bag.

I'm in my zone. I should've never come home, but had I not, there'd be no Tessa.

I don't know how long after, Carter rushes down the stairs and stops at the bottom. "Well, you've done it. She's gone."

My heart drops into my stomach.

"Carter, get your ass up here!" Mom shouts.

I pass him and run up the stairs, two at a time, sliding past Mom in the kitchen. "She's gone?"

She nods and I come to a stop. "I'm afraid so. Her jacket and shoes are missing. I went upstairs to your room and found this."

She hands me a note. It's written on ruled paper torn out of one of my old notebooks.

Tre,

I refuse to come between your family. Not having a family of my own, I know how important family is, something I think maybe you've taken for granted these past years. I wish things were different. I wish we could change a million things, but we can't. I wish my parents wouldn't have died, but they did. I wish my bakery would've survived, but it didn't. I wish Carter wasn't your brother, but he is. Or at least I wish he wasn't the one I was coming for. I wish these things, but at the same time, all of those things are what got me on that plane. They led me to you, and although our time together was brief, I'll never regret it. I hope you find peace with your past because Tre, the love I felt from you this week was the best gift of my life. You're way too good of a person to spend your life alone. Please, love your family, even Carter, because you can't replace them. I'll never forget you or this past week. Merry Christmas.

Love,
   Tessa

My throat burns and my chest feels as if someone is tightening a band around it, making it hard to breathe. I fold the paper and put it in my pocket, sinking into a chair.

"Now do you see why I was warning you?" Carter says from the doorway.

"Carter, give us a minute." Mom points toward the door.

"You see the way he looks at her."

My mom gives him another look, and eventually he leaves. My mom and dad sit across the kitchen table from me.

"So, that's it, huh?" Mom asks. "You're going to sit down?"

I look at her but don't say anything.

"I thought soldiers fought. They fight for our country, for our freedom, for our safety. When do you fight for yourself, Tre? Everyone has their scars, but you have to live and learn from them, not keep picking them open. Let them heal and move on." She leans in across the table. "That woman is amazing, and you know it. So what if she thought Carter was the one? You should thank Carter, because she got on that plane, and your path crossed hers." My mom's voice is rising. It's clear she's lost her patience with me.

"I can't say she's wrong, son," Dad chimes in.

"But—"

"I told her," my mom cuts me off.

My head flies up, eyes wide. "You what?"

"She needed to know. And the fact you hadn't told her tells me all I need to know. You're still harboring guilt or something for what went down all those years ago. You were the innocent party."

"You think I don't know that? But I lost them both because Theresa decided I was her ticket out of this town. Her selfishness ruined my friendship with Toby. She was one of my best friends. How do I trust anyone after that?"

Mom's shoulders sink. "Not all women are like Theresa, honey. And she was young then—a teenager, and teenagers make mistakes." She puts her hands over mine.

"Then what about all the women who ditched their boyfriends as soon they went into basic or when we were on missions? They all found some other guy they wanted."

"That's not Tessa, and deep down, you know that." She squeezes my hand. "The two of you fell hard for one another in a short time. You learned a lot of things about her, and there must have been something that made you trust her enough to open your heart."

I think back to our time on the road. Her dragging me to the gingerbread house, demanding we go to the Eggnog Festival because I love eggnog so much. The way she got me to the hospital when I needed stitches. Her singing in the car. The look in her eyes right after we kissed. She definitely pulled something out of me. She pulled my old self out. The one who wanted to try new things, take risks.

"Oh, he's smiling," Dad says. "That's a good sign."

"I can't lose her," I say, more to myself than them.

"Well, good for you, she's on foot." My dad knocks the table with his knuckles.

I get up, grab the keys to my parents' SUV, throw on a pair

of boots, and leave. I drive down our road, but Tessa's nowhere in sight. I don't know exactly when she left, but she couldn't have gotten very far.

My phone rings and I pull over to answer it. It's my mom's name on the screen.

"I can't find her, Mom." My breath lodges in my throat. What if she's already gone? Called a cab or something?

"I just heard she's at Double D's."

"How did she get downtown already?" I ask.

"You'll find out when you get there, but hurry in case she decides to leave."

"Thanks, Mom," I say.

"You're welcome."

"No, Mom, thank you... for everything... all these years."

"You'll understand when you have kids. I love you and I want you to have everything you want. Parenthood is simple like that."

"Love you too."

We hang up and I get back on the road toward the diner, hoping I can convince Tessa that I am the man for her.

Chapter Twenty-Eight

TESSA

I walk into Double D's, and the man who picked me up waves to the woman behind the counter. "Hey, Debbie."

"I'll be with you two in a minute."

He takes two menus from the counter and sits us next to the main window. When the Uber driver stopped to pick me up without me ordering through the app, I thought it was odd. Even weirder when he offered me a ride into downtown, where the bus depot is for no charge. Said it was his Christmas good deed. Getting in a car with a stranger might not have been the smartest decision, but he looked like a friendly old man and my gut told me I wasn't in any danger.

Then he parked and said the bus depot wouldn't be open for another hour, that they were on lunch, but he'd buy me a meal so I would be full before he sent me on my way. Is this what small-town life is all about?

I slide into the booth and look out at Kent's Restoration. There's a big picture window where you can see the boats being worked on inside.

"It's a craft I wish I knew," the man says, sitting across from me. "Marcus Kent is a resident and well known in the boat world."

"Does he build them from scratch?" I look away from the business to the old man across from me.

"Yeah, a lot of his clients are from the San Francisco area. You know how the rich are. Everyone wants to one-up the other."

Debbie comes over. "Merry Christmas." She rests her hand on my Uber driver's shoulder. "Working, I see?"

"She's my first freebie of the day." He winks. There's something so familiar about his face.

"Isn't he a sweetie? On Christmas Eve, he works for free, taking people anywhere they want to go. The last of the good guys."

"Very nice. Otherwise, I'd still be walking." I smile at her. At least my gut was right that this man wasn't going to kill me.

"Okay, what will you have?" Debbie asks.

"Just a coffee for me. Mary already fed me." He runs his hand in circles over his stomach. "But get the young lady anything she wants."

I peruse the menu of yet another diner. "Can I just have a slice of your pie? And a coffee, please."

"Be right up." She disappears back behind the counter.

"I wish you would have more," he says.

"I'm not terribly hungry, but thank you so much."

"Where are you headed?" He flips his coffee mug up for Debbie, who's returned with coffeepot in hand. I do the same with mine.

"Portland, then back home to New York City."

He frowns. "You'll never get a flight tonight."

"I know. I'm hoping Christmas Day will be less busy and I'll get on standby."

He sighs. "Sounds like a lonely way to spend the holiday."

I am not going into the whole story with this man. There is no pitying Tessa anymore.

"It's just Christmas." I shrug.

He frowns. I raise the coffee cup to my lips as the bell above the door rings. The man across from me smiles and waves to whoever it is, but that's what you expect in a town like this. Everyone knows everyone.

"Tessa!" Tre says.

I whip around to see him walking toward us without a coat or a hat. Just his jeans and sweatshirt, looking gorgeous as he always does.

"What are you doing here?" he asks. He comes to the edge of the table, and I look away from him, out toward Kent's boat restoration place.

"Excuse me, she doesn't seem to want to talk to you," the older gentleman across from me intervenes. What a kind man.

"Please, Tessa. I fucked up."

"And you lost your chance. Now if you wouldn't mind moving along, you're ruining my chances," the old man says.

I turn back to stare at him. He picked me up as in he's trying to pick me up? Who is Mary who fed him then?

"You're too old for her, old man," Tre says.

I stare at Tre with my mouth open. "That wasn't nice." Not something I would ever imagine him saying.

The older gentleman slides out of the booth and pokes Tre in the chest. "I said back off. You clearly don't know how to carry yourself with a woman if she's here by herself."

Tre crosses his arms. "Grandpa, enough. Seriously, I need to talk to her."

The man laughs. "Then stop being a jackass. I'm ashamed for you." He turns to me. "It was a pleasure, Tessa. Give my stupid grandson a second chance. It takes us boys a while

237

sometimes to come around." He winks just like Tre does. That's what was so familiar. "See you at Christmas."

He walks out, saying goodbye to Debbie who's in a fit of laughter.

Tre slides into where his grandpa just was. "First of all, why would you get in a car with a stranger?" He shakes his head. "Never mind. I'm sorry. I'm so fucking sorry for everything."

"Why didn't you tell me about Toby and Theresa?" I frown.

He sighs and grips the back of his neck. "I didn't think it was important, it was so long ago, but I was wrong. Maybe I was embarrassed because of how I reacted. I worried I led her on at some point." He shakes his head. "I'm not sure what my mom told you, but it did mess me up. Made me not trust women. She was dating Toby, and although it put a strain on our friendship, I was happy for them. Then my scholarship to Oregon was announced, and she climbed into my window late one night, telling me how it was always me she wanted and how she could move with me and work while I got my degree and played. How after I went pro, we could get married and stuff. I kept saying what about Toby and she said Toby doesn't have a future, he's not going anywhere. After I denied her advances, she just twisted it around when I went to Toby to tell him the truth."

"But why join the Army?"

"It was a rash decision. I wanted to get as far away from them as possible. I didn't want to become some football star and have more women use me. Losing my best friends, friends I always thought had my best interests at heart, was a hard pill for me to swallow. And then I get to basic, and all these guys keep getting letters from their girlfriends saying they met someone else. It fucked me up."

"I don't want Carter," I say, staring at him in the eye, willing him to see the truth in my words.

He takes my hands, rubbing his thumbs over my knuckles. "I know. My insecurity got the better of me. I thought maybe I was convenient for you on your way to my brother. And that when we arrived here, maybe you regretted us and wished you would've stayed the course on your way to him."

I shake my head. "No. Not at all."

He squeezes my hands. "I know that now. I see how I sabotaged us. But I've never felt so connected to someone. Thinking about losing you, my lungs closed up and I couldn't breathe. I know people will say it's only been a short time, and maybe it's because we were together twenty-four-seven, but I feel as if I know you so well."

I nod. "Me too."

"Come back with me. Spend Christmas with my family."

I bite my bottom lip. "What about your brother? Are you still fighting? I won't come between you two." My voice is strong, sure.

"I still want to kick his ass, but he had a point. I was blind. I didn't see how fortunate I was to have you. I should've been doing everything I could to keep you. Instead, I was driving you away. I'll never do it again. I promise." He slides out of his side of the booth and slides over to mine. "Is this okay?"

"More than okay." I have to resist the urge to lean into him.

"So can I kiss you?"

"You better before I go get your grandpa. By the way, was that Abner the first?"

He takes my head in his hands. "In the flesh. Now shut up so I can kiss you." He bends down and takes my lips. "Come home with me."

I nod and he slides out of the booth, takes my hand, and escorts me out of Double D's.

* * *

When we arrive back at his parents' house, they're arranging the baked sugar cookies on cooling racks.

Gwen hugs me. "Welcome home, first of all. Second, I hope you don't mind. Brynn did yours, and Carter did ours. They're almost cool now. I wasn't sure about your icing."

"I do a royal icing." I look at her ingredients and pull out what I need.

"Want some help?" Tre asks, his arms around my waist and his lips by my ear.

"Look, it's Tre with his tail between his legs." Brynn laughs.

Tre flips her off.

"No giving the bird on Christmas," Gwen says.

"It's technically not Christmas yet," Carter chimes in.

"Listen to your mother," Abner says.

Once I've got everything ready, I ice a cookie with my icing.

"Are you sure you want to be part of this crazy family?" Tre asks me in my ear.

"You're talking to a woman who traveled across the country because of a psychic's advice. I love crazy."

"We should send her a thank you note," Tre says.

"I think we should send Polly one," I counter.

He laughs. I hold out my cookie for him, and he glances at his mom.

"I'd hit you across the back of the head if you didn't try it," Gwen says.

He leans over and chomps down on my sugar cookie. I don't wait for him to tell me which one he prefers, because it doesn't really matter. Although a minute later, he whispers, "Your icing is so good, I want to lick it off your body."

I take that for a win. Not that we're competing or anything.

Actually, I am, because for once I feel as though I'm winning at this game of life.

Epilogue

TESSA

ONE YEAR LATER...

"I cannot believe how big she is," I say.

Abby hesitantly lifts herself up on the couch and stares at Tre. Polly found out Tre's real name after delivering and named her daughter Abby after him.

"It's like she knows," Polly says.

Tre stares at Abby, and I laugh because he looks confused about what he should do.

"You could pick her up and put her on your lap," I offer, but his expression reads scared. The man has put his life on the line in combat, but he doesn't want to pick up a child.

"Abby, come here." I hold out my arms.

She comes over immediately in her cute little Christmas outfit. I lift her and plop her on Tre's lap. He holds her on his lap to steady her, but they each kind of stare at one another.

"So, what's new with you guys?" Polly asks.

We drove to Portland this morning to visit Polly, who now shares an apartment with Gladys. They got along so well and Gladys helped her with the baby and encouraged her to speak to her family, so they found an apartment close to Polly's parents and Gladys's son.

"My partner and I just opened the bakery in Seaside Peaks, the town next to Climax Cove," I say. "I'm partners with a woman who owns a bakery in Climax Cove. She was looking to expand but didn't have the bandwidth, so I run the Mad Hatter location in Seaside Peaks."

"And it had an amazing opening," Tre adds, winking at me.

"That's wonderful."

I nod, still surprised by how different my life is from last year at this time. After Christmas last year, Tre and I weren't sure what we were going to do. He had to settle some things in Georgia, and I didn't have much going on for me in New York, so we decided to take the leap and move to Climax Cove together. It was a bit impulsive and risky, but that's kind of our thing. The only downside is that I'm so far away from Kenzie. But we text and video chat all the time, and she and Andrew have planned a visit for the spring.

"And Tre is coaching football at his old high school."

"Are you guys flying anywhere this holiday season?" Gladys asks.

Tre and I look at one another. Abby gets squirmy and slides off Tre's lap onto the floor, then goes over and plays with some toys Polly put out.

"I'm set on giving Tessa a family holiday all the way through. So we're doing a lot with my parents."

I nod and smile at him, excitement making my stomach feel as if I've eaten too many sugar cookies. "We've cut down our own tree, decorated it, perfected our eggnog recipe, did a cookie exchange, built a snowman, had a snowball fight, and even went through the maze to get pictures with Santa in our little downtown. It's been a lot of fun. Speaking of, you have to bring Abby down next year."

"It's a date," Polly says. "It's like a holiday movie with you two, and if I do recall, I called it when you guys hated one another. "

"That you did, and we are very grateful that you got on that plane," I say.

Tre takes my hand and gives me the look that says we really need to get going. Which I know, but we're so busy I barely get up here to see them.

"We're picking his brother up at the airport, so we should go." I stand from the couch, Tre following suit.

"That's nice of you." Gladys smiles at me, silently asking how that's all going, and I give her a nod.

It's all fine. In fact, Carter is bringing someone home for the holidays.

We all hug and say our goodbyes. Gladys gives us a tin of her sugar cookies for the road. When we get to the car, I wave to them as we drive away.

"Amazing Abby's already so big," I say.

"Yeah, I wouldn't mind having one of those soon."

I laugh because I don't think he can be serious. He looked as though he was dealing with an exotic animal.

We drive to the airport, and Tre's hand is in mine as we illegally wait in the arrival lane to pick up Carter.

"You sure I can't convince you to spend Christmas naked?" Tre says.

I turn to him. "As nice as it sounds, I want Christmas with the whole family."

He groans and lets his head drop back to the headrest. "Fine."

A knock on the window startles me. Carter's there, holding the hand of a pretty blonde. I open my door, and Tre rounds the side to open the back of our SUV.

"Merry Christmas," I say, hugging Carter.

He squeezes me tightly, lifting my feet off the ground.

"Watch it," Tre warns, but it's clear he's joking.

"Hi, I'm Tessa." I put my hand out in front of Carter's girlfriend.

"Nice to meet you." She shakes it and smiles.

Carter gets in between us and introduces us to Luna. When he's done the introductions, the two brothers hug one another.

We drive back to Climax Cove, hearing all about Carter and Luna's meet-cute on the subway. Not nearly as interesting as Tre's and mine.

As soon as we pull into the driveway of Tre's childhood home, the whole family comes rushing out, including Jazzy, to welcome us. Tre and Carter carry in all the presents, and I carry some of the food. Gwen and Abner hug everyone and welcome Luna to the family.

"You're gorgeous. What on earth do you see in him?" Brynn asks Luna.

"And that's my sister," Carter finishes the introductions.

We file into the warmth of the house. The fire roars and I stop and stare at the mantel, where something catches my eye. I set my stuff on the coffee table and walk over, because hanging next to Tre's stocking is a stocking stitched with my name across the top.

"Do you like it?" Gwen comes over and puts her arm around my shoulders.

Tears spill from my eyes. "I love it."

"There's no getting out of this family now."

I laugh and wipe away the tears, giving her a hug.

"We should look inside. I think Santa came a little early for you." Tre comes over and reaches in, pulling out a small box. I shake my head as he falls down on one knee in front of me. "This past year has been the best of my life, Tessa. Last year at this time, I already knew I loved you, but over the past year,

I've fallen more and more in love with you. Make my Christmas wish come true and marry me?"

I nod, covering my mouth.

He tilts his head. "I'm gonna need to hear the word."

"Yes! Yes, I'll marry you!"

He slides the ring on my left ring finger. It's a beautiful round diamond on a silver band.

I jump into his arms when he stands. "I love you so much."

"I was going to propose later tonight during the sugar cookie night, but when you got all emotional over the stocking, I couldn't wait."

"And you all knew?" I look at the rest of the family standing around. *My* family now.

They all nod. Gwen wipes at her tears with Abner holding her close to his side.

"Just so you know, Mom was already done with your stocking before he came up with putting the ring inside," Brynn says.

"I swear to God." Tre bolts toward Brynn and she runs away.

I laugh through my tears, Gwen and Abner coming over to congratulate me. Carter and Luna are next. Tre gets Brynn when she trips on the couch, and he pretends he's going to give her a noogie.

"Are you sure? Now's your time to run," Abner asks me.

Gwen puts her arm around me. "Nope. You're one of us now."

I smile at her, and she smiles back, squeezing me closer.

I finally found my family. And we'll all live happily ever after.

The End

Bonus Epilogue

TWO YEARS LATER

"**B**oarding for flight 267 to JFK," the ticket agent announces over the airport speakers. We're on our way to visit Kenzie and Andrew, and then flying back home to Portland before Christmas. We're cutting it close timewise, but what are the chances we'd end up on some crazy cross country road trip again?

Tre stands when he hears the announcement and grabs our carry-on bags.

"We might as well wait, we're not in first class or anything," I say, flipping through the magazine I bought at the gift shop.

"Says who?" Tre's eyes sparkle with mischief.

I look up, tilting my head and narrowing my eyes. Is he playing with me?

"We can't afford that." I stand and grab the phone out of his hand. Is this why he's been so secretive? Showing the phone for both of our tickets and me just having to show my ID through security?

"I can afford a first class ticket," he says in a voice that makes me think I've offended him.

"I meant more like we're not going to waste our money on first class."

"Well, you didn't get to sit in first class when we first met because of me." He slides his hand in mine, tugging me toward the gate. I barely have time to snatch my purse off my chair.

He's weaving us through the crowd of people waiting to get on the plane. I'm usually one of those people, lingering and waiting for my boarding number to be called. I don't know why I'm always in a rush to get on the plane to begin with.

The ticketing agent scans both of our boarding passes from his phone. She smiles and we walk down the corridor, and right onto the plane.

Tre stops at row four and I laugh, sliding into the window seat. "Did you pick this row on purpose?"

He smiles and puts our carry-ons in the overhead compartment, before taking the aisle seat.

"You're a romantic," I say as the flight attendant comes by and offers me champagne.

I bite my lower lip because I can't have champagne. And if I don't take the glass, Tre is going to figure it out and he's going to cancel our plans for this holiday thinking I can't do everything he's planned. I was going to give him a Christmas present he'll never forget and tell him Christmas morning when we were back in Portland. After we got married in the summer, we both agreed to try right away.

"Tess, take the champagne." Tre stares at me quizzically.

That radar of his is already beeping. If I don't take it, he'll know.

I reach out and take the glass. "Thank you."

She smiles as Tre takes his own, turning toward me while all the other passengers start filing down the aisle.

"I wanted to make this special. How I wish our first time would've gone."

"Then you need to be in coach, and I need to be sitting there." I look at his seat.

He chuckles. "I meant more that we were seated next to one another. I know you wanted to enjoy first class with champagne and..." He bends over and opens his backpack he put under the seat in front of him, pulling out a chenille blanket and small pillow. "Blanket and pillow." Then he lifts his laptop out. "I have two of your favorite holiday movies on here for us to watch."

I run my hand over his cheek. "Thank you."

He opens up the blanket, laying it over my lap, positioning the pillow just so. Then he picks up his glass of champagne. "Cheers."

I tap my glass to his. "Cheers."

And he waits. He doesn't sip his, he just stares at me with a grin.

"What?"

"Take a sip," he nods his head in encouragement.

"Oh... I don't want to get sick on the plane."

"One glass of champagne isn't going to make you sick," he says, continuing to wait for me.

Having no other choice, I figure I'll throw it back his way. "You first. I mean you planned this whole thing, surprising me and everything."

"Nah, ladies first. Dad would kill me, you know that."

I do because his dad would never let chivalry die. In fact, when we told him the story about how Tre let me go back to coach, he was really mad. Like legit not talking to Tre even though I said how it had to be that way otherwise we wouldn't have gotten together. It all happened for a reason. Cause and effect.

But Tre isn't going to sip first and I'm going to have to do it.

"Oh." I point but he doesn't turn his head. "I thought it was Polly for a second."

"We'd know if she was going to be on a plane." He eyes the drink and looks back at me.

I blow out a breath. "How long have you known?"

He laughs, downs his champagne and laughs some more. "Did you really think you could hide it from me?"

"Yes." I'm adamant because I'm early. I just took a test last week. No one knows at all, and I threw the test away in the dumpster at work so I wouldn't accidentally spoil the surprise.

"You missed your period," he whispers. "Did you think I wouldn't notice?"

"A normal man wouldn't have," I grumble.

He chuckles and tucks a strand of my hair behind my ear. "I'm not a normal man."

I raise both eyebrows.

"I was in the military, I mean. I seek out information. I'm trained to notice things."

"So you keep track of my periods?" I ask, disappointed because I wanted to surprise him.

"Well, first off, I'm usually the one who empties the trash-cans, and one day I realized I hadn't seen all the girly stuff in a while. And this week, you said you were going to make smoothies for breakfast instead of coffee every morning. And three out of the five nights you fell asleep at eight."

"Maybe I was just tired from my long day of baking. It is the holiday season after all." I mock offense.

Tre slides his hand under my blanket, cradling my stom-ach. "Tell me," he whispers.

I put my hand over his and squeeze. "I'm pregnant."

He leans over and places his lips to mine, drawing back, he leaves his lips millimeters away. "You're going to be the best mom ever."

"And you're going to be an amazing dad."

"I love you," he whispers, placing his lips on mine once more.

He rests his forehead against mine and we just sit there in our own little world, relishing the fact that we're going to be parents.

"Drink the champagne, it's non-alcoholic," he says, digging through his bag again.

My mouth drops open. "What? How?" I have so many questions.

"You do know you're the least observant person I know," he says.

And we're back at it.

"That's insulting."

"Not when you're married to me. I'll always make sure you're on the right track." He winks. That sexy move still makes me wet.

"Well, aren't I the lucky one." I playfully roll my eyes.

He turns to look at me. "You are," he deadpans but immediately smirks and I lightly smack him on the shoulder. "So, this is our change of itinerary." He hands me a piece of paper. "Once I figured out your secret, I changed some things around."

Without looking, I inhale before saying something I might regret. "We're changing nothing. I'm only pregnant."

"I know, but..."

I open up the sheet prepared to grab a red marker and cross out all the boring shit he's going to fill my day with instead of all the fun we had planned, but as I read through it I realize that nothing has changed. I look over at him and he's grinning like goon. "Tell me I'm the world's best husband."

I place my hand on his cheek, his five o'clock stubble already in full effect. "Someone need an ego boost?" He stares at me. "Thank you."

"You're welcome."

The attendant comes by and takes our glasses. I snuggle into Tre's shoulder as best I can in the seat. The lights turn down and the pilot says we're ready for takeoff.

Tre kisses my forehead and I already feel my eyelids slipping shut before the plane gets off the ground.

Sometime later, I wake up with a jolt, looking around the quiet plane. Tre is passed out next to me, as are most of the other passengers. I'm not sure what woke me up, probably mild turbulence, so I lay my head back down.

"You okay?" Tre mumbles.

"Sorry, just woke for a second. Go back to sleep."

He stretches his arm over my lap and rests his head on mine that's now on his shoulder again.

The plane drops in the air and I jolt up, knocking his head. "Did you feel that?" I ask him.

"It's just turbulence. A lot of storms and stuff this time of year." He's groggy and sleepy still.

And I believe him until the pilot gets on the speaker announcing, "I'm sorry passengers, we have to make an emergency landing. Nothing to worry about, a precaution more than anything. Just sit tight and we'll be on the ground in about fifteen minutes."

Tre and I both lock eyes. Not again.

Cockamamie Unicorn Ramblings

Happy holidays first and foremost. We do hope you loved Tessa and Tre's journey to love.

Writing a holiday book in July is rough, even when immersing yourself in Christmas songs and movies. It's even harder when life gets in the way. Unfortunately, while writing this story, we both lost someone close to us in our families.

If you watch any holiday movie, it usually has to do with some aspect of family. Whether someone doesn't have one (like Tessa) or someone doesn't get along with them or is returning home to them (like Tre). Regardless family can be a major part of the storyline and it was for us after plotting.

Here we found ourselves writing a heroine who had lost everything and only really wanted a family for Christmas. All the while we were both grieving that this year on Christmas there would be a chair not filled by our loved one.

As a result, there were three chapter ones written, two chapter twos at one point because we couldn't decide where to start the book, along with many conversations between us, saying let's start here, no there, maybe here. In the end we changed it to a short prologue after deciding that we needed to get Tessa and Tre on page together right away. It was a rough start for not only Tessa and Tre but us too. In the end after two deadline extensions, the book got written.

Personal note from Rayne: This was the hardest rough draft I've ever had to write. And not because of the characters or storyline. I loved them both. But grieving the unexpected loss of my brother while writing a Christmas story was harder than I imagined. Had I been writing our small town or sports series, my mind would still have been preoccupied yes, but not constantly reminded about things I'll miss experiencing with him in the years to come. With Christmas comes traditions and every family has their own memories that are shared for years. I don't come from a big family and we moved a lot, so, most years it was only me, my brother, my sister and my parents. So, this Christmas, I'll eat the cheese kolaczky even though I love the almond, I'll make sure your childhood paper plate ornament sits highest on the tree, and I'll make a sugar cookie with your initial and decorate it.

Whoops I almost forgot... Tessa is my oldest niece's name, my brother's biological daughter. We usually shy away from names of our close family members, but since Tessa was named in Single and Ready to Jingle already, we had no choice but to use it. My first time ever having a main character with the name of a family member. A tad weird in the sexy times to be truthful.

As always, we have a lot of people to thank for getting this book into your hands!

Nina and the entire Valentine PR team.

Cassie from Joy Editing for line edits. Thank you for being so accommodating with the deadline for this one.

My Brother's Editor for line edits and proofreading. So much love for pushing this one through on a rush.

Hang Le for the cover and branding it to match Single and Ready to Jingle.

All the bloggers who read, review, share and/or promote us.

The Piper Rayne Unicorns in our Facebook group who are always our biggest cheerleaders!

Every reader who took the time to read this book! Thank you for granting us your most precious resource—time. We don't take that lightly.

We hope you all have a wonderful holiday season and new year!

xo,
Piper & Rayne

About Piper & Rayne

Piper Rayne is a USA Today Bestselling Author duo who write "heartwarming humor with a side of sizzle" about families, whether that be blood or found. They both have e-readers full of one-clickable books, they're married to husbands who drive them to drink, and they're both chauffeurs to their kids. Most of all, they love hot heroes and quirky heroines who make them laugh, and they hope you do, too!

Also by Piper Rayne

Bedroom Games

Cold as Ice

On Thin Ice

Break the Ice

Box Set

Charity Case

Manic Monday

Afternoon Delight

Happy Hour

Blue Collar Brothers

Flirting with Fire

Crushing on the Cop

Engaged to the EMT

White Collar Brothers

Sexy Filthy Boss

Dirty Flirty Enemy

Wild Steamy Hook-up

The Rooftop Crew

My Bestie's Ex

A Royal Mistake

The Rival Roomies

Our Star-Crossed Kiss

The Do-Over

A Co-Workers Crush

Made in United States
North Haven, CT
19 November 2023

44253487R00168